Lizzi

The Life
of
Grace Harper Maxwell

Lizzie Collins

ISBN: 9798839646018

Dedication

To all those with Grace's spirit of adventure. May
you achieve your goals.

Acknowledgement

I would like to acknowledge the bravery and strength of those who worked so hard to open up an entirely new continent in such a ridiculously short period of time. They were people with Grace's admirable determination to succeed.

Chapter One
The Seventh Circle of Hell

The sight of the Statue of Liberty should have been a relief to our poor aching bones but it wasn't.

The day we sailed towards New York harbor was so foggy we had difficulty making out even the tip of her torch and it was so cold. The damp went right through to my skin.

Addie's nose had dripped continually since we shipped out of Liverpool, horrible dirty place full of incomprehensible voices. Some English accents even I found well-nigh impossible to make out.

We'd traipsed backwards and forwards from Yorkshire a dozen times, organizing papers extra to our shipping tickets, signing this or that document, and finally we were all set.

The only fares we could afford were in steerage, jammed like rats in a trap between brats with rank diapers and men with dubious intent, women screaming and crying - all jibber-jabbering in a dozen different languages.

Pickpocketing was rife aboard the ship which brought us across. I thanked God I'd had the sense to sew our meagre savings into our knickers before we left, keeping just what we needed to hand.

I tended not to be a sympathetic sister – Addie was two years older than me, so I was aggrieved she wasn't looking after me instead.

We were much of a size, small and slight, but where she was delicate, blue-eyed, and ladylike, I was wiry and tended to speak my mind without much thought for the consequences.

Addie – fine light hair, high cheekbones, hand-span waist. Me - grim expression, good teeth and nails. Not a stretch of the imagination to guess which one of us would attract the boys.

You can't sail straight into New York harbor, it's too shallow, so they have to send boats out to take you to enter Ellis Island. The complex of buildings, through a sea mist, a mile out and with your eyes screwed half shut could be construed as resembling an Italianate palace.

So there we were like sardines in a tin can, waiting to be decanted into cattle sheds.

I saw them separating families to slide them through different counters, so I lashed our wrists together with a cord from my hair and tied it good and tight.

And such a cacophony of noise! A babbling of tongues! A diversity of dress. I'd always thought Americans were like us.

We had thermometers pushed from one person to the next without cleaning shoved in our mouths, and merely glanced at. We avoided thankfully the awful chalk marking to say we had a dangerous illness, or worse were mentally defective. Then we were pushed none too gently to the next queue. Most got through, some were led off – I'd no idea to where.

We'd been stuck all over onboard ship with syringes which could have contained bubonic plague for all we knew. Then they gave us a card to say we didn't have what we'd probably picked up from the inoculations. We were issued with the golden ticket – well a pretty tatty poor-quality card anyway - which we'd to present at a plethora of counters once inside.

Then questions, questions and more questions. Endless jabbering and stamping of forms, coughing and arguing. One thing was for sure - once I got in, no way on God's good green earth would I ever leave. The Americans had got us – well, me anyway – for good, whether they liked it or not.

I was sixteen and Addie was eighteen, and we both looked like scarecrows before we got through. My fingers were so numb with cold I could hardly untie our tether.

The queue for the money exchange was a much happier experience. Everyone there had gotten through, so they felt American already. Ha! What a joke.

It wasn't long before our tickets were examined, and we were hustled off to Pennsylvania Station. There, we were standing above a concourse so different from any we'd seen in England, it might have been on another planet. It felt like we'd fallen into the Seventh Circle of Hell.

We stood at the top of a steep flight of marble-faced concrete steps and gazed below us in horror. The noise was deafening and people were running backwards and forwards trying to locate family members. Everyone was shouting in a multitude of languages. Touts were shoving wads of tickets to every possible destination in the faces of people who had no hope of comprehending what they were saying. Women and children were sitting on packages of their belongings, wailing loudly. Damn if I wasn't nearly sobbing myself - Addie certainly was.

I grabbed her hand, tiptoed down the staircase, and skirted the wall being careful to avoid the crowds.

God was smiling on us. We found a tout taking a break, sitting on a bench about to bite into a door-step sandwich he'd removed from inside his hat. He pointed to a legitimate ticket office and advised us to go there. I thought that was good of him since he'd have lost commission on a sale, but perhaps we didn't look as if we had the price of the fare.

We'd had the promise of a job with a lady in a country area of Connecticut. The employment agent in Liverpool had said we were the best of a bad bunch, so we'd have to do.

Once we arrived in the United States, I was thanking heaven we only had to travel fifty miles to our employment, and not the near thousand miles to Chicago or three thousand to California. I'd also heard there was a great disaster near Chicago. It was something to do with farms, but I knew nothing else.

Once we got settled, I meant to find out absolutely all I could. I intended to make America my home. I would do whatever was needed to get my naturalization papers. At least I could read and write in English, which I understood put me several rungs up the ladder before I even started.

I confess I looked forward to a bright new future and didn't give much thought to what we'd left behind.

Addie was a pain in the neck. I never knew a small human body could contain so much water.

Chapter Two

From Yorkshire to Connecticut

Our new employer was called Mrs. Hamilton.

Her chauffeur picked us up from the station in Danbury. We found him leaning against her gleaming Cadillac and grinning, his peaked cap slewed to one side. He was holding a torn off piece of card with 'HARPER' written on it and chewing gum with his mouth opened wide enough for me to see his tonsils. He introduced himself as Lon and offered his pack of gum. Addie gripped my hand and moved behind me, but I stepped forward and tentatively took a piece. I'd had it once before - it was horrible. But I thought if it was offered in friendship, I should at least show willing.

We drove off faster than the railway train could go, examining our surroundings with eyes like gobstoppers.

The sun was setting, lending fire to the dazzling autumn leaves, and turning the lawns to emerald.

My first impression of America was that the houses were all miles apart, very large and made of planks, whereas we were more used to brick, and occasionally stone on the posher buildings. Mostly they were painted white or blue and had gables in odd places, unlike the symmetrical buildings at home.

We pulled up a sweeping gravel drive and Lon drew up before a studded door which looked as if it belonged on a castle. A large lady with grey hair and a wart on her chin stood on the steps, as Lon held open the car door for us to get out.

He winked broadly at her and dumped our scant belongings on the drive, before revving the engine loudly and driving off round the side of the house.

I stood up straight and stuck my hand out bravely.

"How do you do, Mrs. Hamilton" I said, tucking behind my ear a stray lock of hair which had worked loose. "I am Grace Harper, and this is my sister Adelaide. We are very happy to know you."

A little voice from behind her gave a soft titter.

"Lord love you child," she said in a broad Irish accent, "I'm not herself. I'm Mrs. Doyle – Mrs. Hamilton's housekeeper. Mrs. Hamilton's away in DC visiting family." *DC?*

She sniffed as if the relatives didn't entirely meet with her approval - or perhaps she just had a cold.

Despite her high standing, she picked up our two bags with beefy arms and dumped them on a waiting servant, whose knees wobbled under the impact.

"And a fine welcome to Danbury House, to you both.

"You'll be taking them to Maggie's old room. Don't drop anything this time," said Mrs. Doyle to her underling.

By now, Addie and I were propping each other up like bookends with exhaustion, so Mrs. Doyle, bless her heart, said:

"Bed now me beauties. Time enough tomorrow for our little chat."

I nearly expired with relief.

"Thank you, Mrs. Doyle. You have been very kind."

Our savior had our belongings taken away and burnt, handling them with care as if they had fleas, which they probably had.

She showed us up several staircases to the smartest little room I ever saw and folded a key each into our hands.

"You'll be letting me know in the morning if there's anything else you require," she said, and marched off downstairs again.

The room wasn't huge as the rest of the house seemed to be, but it contained two little beds with soft rosy blankets and patchwork covers, hand-worked in a multitude of pastel shades and patterns. It was a little place of our own to call home, and by far the most luxury we had ever seen.

It was a world away from our childhood in Northern England, with its factory chimneys and blackened brickwork. Halifax may have provided full employment, but it also created emphysema, tuberculosis, and cancer. There was no pristine clean air like Danbury.

Next door to our little haven was a room with a good-sized shower cubical, which I understood was to be ours on condition we kept it clean.

I'd never seen one before. Addie eyed it dubiously. We didn't bathe much at home - it was too cold, and heating water on our range was a long and expensive business. One bathful had to serve an entire family, so the last one often came out grubbier than he went in.

I dragged Addie into the cubical and we scrubbed each other until our hair squeaked and our fingers wrinkled. If

I live to be a hundred, I will never again experience such bliss.

When we'd dried ourselves, we found a couple of cotton nightdresses for us over a chair back. That prompted me to examine the little chest of drawers between out beds. It was full of neatly folded underwear and changes of uniform with a little note saying:

> *"All your clothes are to be changed daily and soiled items placed in the laundry receptacle on the landing. Newly laundered items will be placed outside your door (which must be kept locked when unoccupied). Any questions should be addressed to Mrs. Doyle personally."*

For the whole of my life, I was able to repeat from memory that little note of instruction. It stuck in my mind mostly because I'd no idea what a receptacle was.

I looked at Addie and announced:

"Well, that's it…. we're not English any more - we're Americans. Or at least – we will be!"

On that point I was determined. Addie quailed at the sight of my clenched teeth. Why in God's name had she come?

Then I fell on my bed pole-axed and slept until daybreak.

Chapter Three
A Library and Lessons Learned

The following day had its ups and downs. Mostly downs, since we had no idea what our duties were. We crept about like little mice, until a busy Mrs. Doyle realized we'd just been abandoned.

"And where's that useless Colleen?" she huffed, "Jenny, where are ye?"

It's worth mentioning I think that Americans had the courtesy to use Christian names with junior staff members, whereas in England I'd have just been 'Harper'.

Jenny came running through the kitchen door, skidding to a halt across the waxed floor, at the same time pulling straight her mop-cap.

One of the kitchen maids came for Addie. It was the first time we'd ever been parted, and I felt oddly vulnerable.

Mrs. Doyle near skinned Jenny alive for her laziness, and pushed her out of the door, at the same time dragging me after her by the wrist. Jenny was glowering at me as if I'd personally planned her downfall.

"Now," intoned 'herself'. "Show Grace how to lay a fire in the first floor sitting room, polish the brass and beeswax the fine furniture. We'll come to the carpets later. I want this done – and properly mind – before the dinner gong. Now be about your business instead of mooning about the kitchen door with that useless good-for-nothing Jimmy Dixon.

I learned later that Jimmy Dixon delivered meat from the butcher in Danbury, and Jenny thought of him as her

10

beau. At the time I'd no idea what that was, only that it didn't sound American.

I came across Addie in the kitchen of Danbury House, when we sat down with the other servants to a nourishing dinner of mashed potatoes, some green vegetable I'd never seen before, and gammon, followed by the most scrumptious apple-tart I ever tasted.

We'd never eaten so well at home. Sometimes we went to bed with empty stomachs through the bad times, when Dad got laid off and the mills weren't hiring.

My hands were so raw from 'Brasso' I could hardly hold my knife and fork.

Addie'd been peeling potatoes all morning. She looked dazed, but then she usually did if given more than one job to do at a time. She was easily bullied and rarely found the courage to say no, so it was a situation well known to her. And me.

As we rose to leave for our evening duties, Mrs. Doyle motioned us to sit again, and told us Mrs. Hamilton would be returning from Washington in two days' time. By then, the house had to be scrubbed from top to bottom.

Adam Smith, the youngest of the four under-gardeners, whispered she was very particular.

The house was beautiful, with highly polished furniture – an odd mixture of antique and modern. It had so many rooms I kept getting lost, but one momentous day I found the library.

It was a large and bright room with high ceilings and French windows which opened onto a sloping lawn. The

11

whole room smelled like paradise to me: a mixture of scent from heavy-headed China roses which festooned a trellis next to the windows, beeswax and old parchment.

In the center of a book-lined wonderland, stood a large table with two neat piles of leather-bound volumes, with gold-edged pages. I ran my fingers over their plush covers.

I was so intent on admiring the books that I failed to hear Jenny, until her hand came down hard on my shoulder. I jumped and turned to find us almost nose to nose.

"You shouldn't be in here," she snarled. "This isn't your room to clean – its mine. Now clear off and don't let me see you in here again, or I'll go straight to Mrs. Hamilton."

Well, that was a lie for a start. Mrs. Doyle would fire her on the spot. But I did take her point. I already knew the servants were very jealous of their own domains, and this wasn't mine.

I returned to my duties and went to the closet in the kitchen corridor to collect a holder of cleaning items to take up to the first-floor drawing room.

As I was bent over searching the bottom shelf for a block of beeswax, I came close to landing face first on the stone floor from a slap to my bottom.

I turned round; my fist clenched ready to deal with the culprit. I'd to pull my punch when I realized it was Peter Novak, Mrs. Doyle's opposite number with the male staff. The complacent toad was grinning all over his face. We both knew I could do nothing about it, but I could bide my time.

I tapped my foot and scowled.

"My time will come," I promised grimly.

He chortled and walked off – arrogant bastard.

Meanwhile, I'd a drawing room and first floor bathroom to clean for Mrs. Hamilton's return. On my way up the servant's staircase, lugging my caddy in one hand and a broom under my other arm, I idly wondered who Mr. Hamilton was. No one had so much as mentioned him.

Lon had collected Mrs. Hamilton from Pennsylvania Station in New York. She arrived home in a flurry of gloves, travel coats, fur wraps and perfume. Lon tipped his hat and disappeared respectfully, most likely to polish the car,

I don't know what I was expecting – probably some rotund, middle-aged matron – but I wasn't prepared for the Faery Queen the whole line-up of servants bowed or curtsied to.

I would guess she was in her mid-thirties, with finger-waved blond curls, bobbed short in the fashion of the day. Her eye makeup would have done Max Factor proud and accentuated her stunning violet eyes. Everything she was wearing matched everything else, including her suede clutch purse and high heeled shoes. Only the fox fur was different. She walked with a swaggering hip-swing I'd only ever seen in the movies. She was…. sensational.

She smiled vaguely and wafted past us in a haze of Chanel to the salon, kicked off her shoes and examined a ladder in her stocking. She lit a cigarette from the box on a low table and slumped wearily back in her chair. Her cheeks virtually disappeared with the force of her initial drag.

"Doyle, have one of the girls fetch me a drink. Dinner will be in an hour's time. I'm famished."

Mrs. Doyle bobbed a curtsey and herded the kitchen staff off at the double.

Once Mrs. Hamilton had swallowed her glass of Scotch, she daintily climbed the steps to her private suite, swinging her shoes in her left hand. The rest of the staff, looking more determinedly busy than I had ever seen them, dispersed.

Chapter Four

'Mighty' and the Sticky Situation

That Friday, there being nothing left to scrub or polish, Mrs. Hamilton gave us the evening off. We learned from some of the other girls, there was a dance at the Starlight Lounge in Danbury that very evening. I wasn't averse to kicking my heels up, so I decided to join them. Addie tagged along.

The Starlight Lounge turned out to be a new dancehall, and the band playing was pretty 'hot' – American for good, I learned.

I was expecting foxtrots and quicksteps like at the local Palais at home, so I was not prepared for what was to come.

Of course, I'd seen Fred Astaire and Ginger Rodgers at the pictures, but I'd just thought that was for Hollywood. These 'kids' frightened the hell out of me. I stood amazed, watching them dance the Swing, which I thought I might like to learn. Then two of them took center floor and began to do the Lindy Hop. Everyone else moved to the side, as well they might.

I can truly say I was speechless. It was like a gymnastics performance to music. The girl was swung up-side-down, over his shoulder, through his legs. She was twirled, whirled, dragged and pushed until all I could see was a blur. How the hell didn't she choke on her gum?

The girls I'd come with were mostly servants of Mrs. Hamilton's, although there were a few from other nearby houses. They thought the expression on my face hilarious.

"Here – have a smoke and relax," said Matty, a tall girl with what I was told was a Brooklyn accent. She held out a pack of cigarettes. I'd never done that either. I took one and lit it, holding it all wrong, burning my fingers and coughing immoderately. By this time Joan, a kitchen maid who worked alongside Addie, was laughing so much she'd to hold her sides.

"You need some education," she eventually managed to splutter. "When Ma Doyle gives us time off again, we'll show you….," she paused. "Just about everything by the looks of it."

She was as good as her word and spent the next couple of days off teaching me how to smoke and dance, but thankfully not the Lindy Hop. I drew the line there although she insisted on showing me some of the simpler steps. I even stopped coughing with a cigarette. In my mind, I became Mrs. Hamilton, and felt very sophisticated. Now all I had to do was learn to walk like Mae West.

The evening finished at ten-thirty and the last dance was a slow glide.

A hand touched me tentatively on the shoulder and its owner said:

"May I please have the pleasure of this dance?"

Even a posh English lord wouldn't say that!

I took a good look at him. He was a hand taller than me with hair color I could only guess was fair, though through all the Brylcream it was hard to tell. He was wearing a suit which fit well and would have looked good if it hadn't been short a button. There was a sore-looking spot on his nose.

"Sure. Why not?," I said with a shrug.

He took my hand onto the dance-floor and held me closely as he guided us in a slow dance. I was amazed to find he was pretty good, proficient enough to make up for my deficiencies, because I was mediocre at best.

At the end, the band wound down and girls started picking up their coats from the cloak room. He and I stood and chatted while the crowds dispersed.

I learned his name was Alec Maxwell and he was about to enter his senior year at Canterbury – *wasn't that in England?* - and hoped to go to study medicine at some institute in Boston. That made him a year older than me. He continued:

"The situation abroad is a bit sticky at the moment though, what with the English and Germans. I hope we don't get dragged in again."

This was news to me.

"What situation's that? I only arrived a couple of months ago and I've been a bit preoccupied since then."

He raised his eyebrows in surprise.

"I can hear you're English. I was hoping you'd be able to tell me some more."

"Is that why you asked me to dance? Well, thanks a lot."

Addie chose that moment to tug on my sleeve. I stuck my nose in the air and left him standing at the edge of the dance floor. I was seething.

Matty and the other girls were waiting for me outside.

"See you were pounced on by 'Mighty' Maxwell. Good luck. What did he want?"

"He'd picked up on my being English and wanted to know what was going on between the British and Germans. He seemed to think I'd know something."

"You should have stuck around. His dad's some rich doctor-type. They have a big house in the country. He usually hangs out with the country club girls. Don't know what he was doing getting down and dirty with the local trash here," snorted Matty and blew a smoke ring.

"What's Canterbury? He said he was at school there."

"It's a private school in Milford for rich kids. They all turn out to be doctors or lawyers and such," said Joan.

I lay awake that night studying a cobweb which had appeared on the ceiling above my bed and thinking.

Rich, right age, intelligent, and most important of all, American. I could sew on buttons and put up with acne, I could do worse. Perhaps I could convince him I was worth a shot.

I turned over and spent a restless night dreaming of explosions and burning buildings.

Chapter Five

The Faery Queen

The following morning, I was first down to breakfast, finished my chores double quick and made a dash for the library, before Jenny could catch me. I was out of the servant's dining-room before she'd even arrived, so there was a good chance.

Alec Maxwell had worried me, and I needed to find out what exactly was happening back in England. After my last visit I knew I shouldn't be there at all, but the desire to put my mind at rest overcame my fear.

In the library on my first foray, I'd noticed a rack next to a leather armchair. Glancing surreptitiously over my shoulder I rapidly leafed through the newspapers, until I found one with a banner headline

"Britain and Germany – Can it Happen Again?"

I heard footsteps down the hall, so I rapidly folded the newspaper and stuffed it down the back of my skirt. Oh God, Jenny!

"Damn! You again…. you're for it this time. I'm taking you to Mrs. Doyle!"

"You do that!" I said with a bravado I didn't feel, and while trying to stuff the newspaper further down my knickers.

"What have you got there?" she demanded and swung me round roughly, catching me in the act.

"You damn little thief!"

She got hold of me by the arm and dragged me down the servants' stairs to Mrs. Doyle's office looking smug.

"I warned you about her Ma'am. Just caught her in the act of stealing this from the library," she exclaimed to empty air, waving the newspaper around in triumph.

No Mrs. Doyle. The room was empty. Jenny stamped her foot at being thwarted.

From her enthusiasm, it was clear to see she couldn't read. It was pretty poor evidence, easily explained. Her opinion carried zero weight, but I turned to see Mr. Novak, grinning like a Cheshire Cat, standing in the doorway.

"What have we here, Jenny?," he smiled, hands tucked behind his back, swinging backwards and forwards on the balls of his feet. He couldn't have been more delighted if he'd bought the winning ticket at the Kentucky Derby.

I went as red as a beet and stuttered, handing over the now-tatty newspaper I had stashed in my underwear.

"It's the Washington Post. I wanted to read about the British and Germans. My family lives near Liverpool and I wanted to know what was going on."

"Two problems with that," chortled Mr. Novak. "One, you got caught, and two, you can't read. Seems to me you are a plain and simple thief, like Jenny says."

I was just about to express my outrage, when I had second thoughts and decided to keep the fact I could read to myself.

"Well, I've no time to stand arguing. Mrs. Hamilton can sort you out. After you've seen her, no dawdling - go pack your things. You'll be on the street by supper time. And to show I'm not a vindictive man, I'll have your sister pack some food to take with you."

He put a heavy hand on my shoulder, and whistling, led me down the parquet flooring of the hall to the room where Mrs. Hamilton wrote her letters, and her bookkeeper did the accounts. I supposed you could call it her office except Mrs. Hamilton was far too chic to have any such thing.

By the time Novak rapped on the door, I was close to tears. He looked hideously smug.

"Yes? Enter," said a preoccupied voice.

Mrs. Hamilton was seated at a small walnut desk, shoes kicked off and with a fountain pen between her fingers. She looked up as we entered.

"Mrs. Hamilton, Ma'am. Could you please deal with a matter of discipline above my authority?" *Ugh, he was just so smarmy.*

"Yes, go on."

"This little minx was caught by one of the other maids stealing this from the library."

He carefully placed the paper on a corner of the desk and stood back. Marcia Hamilton put down her pen and picked up the paper, opening it and turning it this way and that. She sighed.

"What of it? It's an old newspaper. Hardly the family silver."

That took the wind out of Novak's sails. It was clear he was expecting me to be sacked on the spot.

"You may leave us, Novak. Go."

21

She swung back round on her chair and continued to write, tucking her curtain of silky curls behind one ear.

Mr. Novak left in high dudgeon. Mrs. Hamilton swiveled back round and looked me up and down.

"I don't know you, do I?"

I curtsied, feeling overawed by this glamorous woman.

"No Ma'am. I arrived from England while you were in DC." *Sounded savvier than Washington.*

"What exactly have you been up to, to get Novak's panties in a twist?"

"I took the paper from the library without asking. I was going to put it back."

"You can read then?" she raised a perfectly plucked eyebrow in surprise. It seemed to be taken for granted that girls in service were ignorant.

Mrs. Hamilton paused to light a cigarette with a dainty cloisonné lighter.

"Well, what to do with you?" she said considering me, head on one side.

"I'll go pack my things, Ma'am. Mr. Novak said I should be out of here by supper-time."

"Novak? Oh, don't mind him – I don't."

I suddenly saw her vulnerable side. She was actually very sweet but put on a brusque manner when dealing with the likes of her houseman. She didn't seem born to her role.

I knew Novak was listening, so I made a point of making it to the door in two strides and opening it wide, so he stumbled inside. When I thought of it afterwards, I was horrified. I had interfered between my employer and a senior servant. I just hoped Mrs. Hamilton put it down to ignorance and youth.

"Novak, Miss…?

"Harper, Ma'am. Grace Harper."

"Grace is to be allowed access to the library whenever she wishes." She cast serious eyes on me. "Except in working hours, that is. Now go away Novak."

He left – properly this time.

"Incidentally, Grace. Why did you want the newspaper?"

"Because of the trouble in Europe, Ma'am."

"Ah yes. You're English."

Mrs. Hamilton lifted her crystal tumbler of Scotch and, silently if unsteadily, drank my health.

I really did try to carry on as normal, but Novak and Jenny together presented a united front it was difficult to ignore.

I didn't forget to gloat whenever I entered the library, and made sure to step into the garden, leaving a muddy footprint on the carpet for Jenny to clean. Sometimes small pleasures are the sweetest.

But Mr. Novak picked me up on everything. I just stayed out of his way. If Mrs. Doyle knew what was going on, she said nothing.

I kept myself apprised of the situation in England. We'd left behind our Dad – mum had died after the youngest baby was born – two children older than me, James who was always called Gem, and Adelaide who was with me here in America. Then there were three younger ones: Edith who had been fourteen when we left, Robbie eleven and the baby Freddie, just eight years old.

I always told the Americans we lived near Liverpool as it's the only place in the north of England they knew, but we actually lived in Halifax, a town of woolen mills and coal mines in Yorkshire. It wasn't pretty, all the buildings being covered in a thick layer of soot, and there was a great deal of poverty, but Yorkshire folks are full of humor, and can laugh at adversity which is a rare trait.

I was born into the last round of hostilities between England and Germany. I'd a cousin who died in the mud and blood of the Somme in France, and another Tommy, my Uncle Albert's oldest, who died of fever near Ypres in Belgium.

Everybody had someone who didn't make it through. Many were worse off than us. Our neighbor lost her husband and two sons. There being no breadwinner left to take care of them, they ended up in the Poor House. We lost touch with them after that.

I got an awful feeling in the pit of my stomach when I thought my family might have to suffer the whole thing over again.

But that was the old world. I determined to make a place for us in the new wide-open spaces and clean air of Connecticut. Or anywhere else in America, come to that. The whole continent was my oyster. Mr. Novak could go jump off a cliff.

Chapter Six

The Suitor

It must have been half a year later when Mrs. Hamilton sent me to buy some ribbon from the milliner to tie, God help us, round the throat of her ghastly little Pomeranian, Cherry.

As I walked past the end of Jacob's Yard, a dark cubbyhole of a place off Main Street, a hand shot out and grabbed me by the jacket, whisking me clean off my feet.

"What in the name of all that's holy do you think you're doing?" I yelled wrenching myself free and landing a great clout on the ear of the idiot beside me.

He reeled backwards and ended up in an untidy heap in a puddle. I turned to leave while I still could.

"Grace…. Gracie. Don't go!"

I turned round and peered through the gloom at the figure measuring his length on the paving stones of Jacob's Yard. My Lord, it was 'Mighty' Maxwell! Wasn't that just a turn up for the books?

I helped him to his feet, and he did his best to dry off the seat of his pants with his handkerchief.

"Grace, please….," he yanked at my arm again, so I stamped on his foot. I was getting seriously annoyed. "Please will you take this to Adelaide for me?"

He held out an envelope with my sister's Sunday name on it in flowing script.

"Adelaide? ADDIE? What the hell do you want with Addie?"

"I want so badly to speak to her Grace, but I can't get anywhere near her. She never gets to leave the house alone. She's not like you," said Alec, his boyish features distressed.

"Your Dad might have a deal to say about this. Aren't you supposed to be going to Harvard - or somewhere – next year? Didn't you want to be a doctor - or something?"

I was scraping the bottom of the barrel here. I was short on detail but I thought I was doing pretty well, given that we'd had one conversation on the subject six months ago.

"Yes, I am… I do. Well, I thought I did but I can't bear the thought of leaving her."

"For crying out loud…" I suddenly realized the only first name I could remember for him was 'Mighty'. "Say, what's your first name? I've forgotten."

"Alexander Maxwell but I prefer Alec."

"Does your mother know you've changed your name?" I asked derisively.

This guy was such a sap. Was he worshiping Addie from afar? If he'd ever met her, she sure as hell hadn't said anything to me.

"Oh, give it here," I snapped, left and stomped about my errands.

Poor Alec, I'm not known for my sympathetic nature as I think I already said. Addie was usually on the receiving end of my temper, and this was probably going to be another of those times.

Of course, with my bad mood, I'd got the shade of ribbon wrong. Poor Cherry - must remember to step on her paw. Mrs. Hamilton sighed and forgave me.

My chores as a parlor maid were sometimes long but not usually arduous, and much to Mr. Novak's fury I was often able to scoot off to the library. I'd learned it was wise not to go until after our tea to avoid Jenny. It was beyond my ability not to continue my small annoyances and leave a fingerprint on the pristine window, or a book askew on the top shelf,

Once I'd waded through the collected works of Charles Dickens, which was a matter of determination, and managed a good bit of Walt Whitman, I suddenly realized I was gradually beginning to fill some of the gaps in my learning. I'd attended a primary school but nothing since.

There were books on the sciences but, except for a bit of curiosity about human reproduction, I found I wasn't particularly interested. Literature was another matter.

I'd asked Mrs. Hamilton if I could occasionally take a book to my room to finish reading it. She was surprised but usually agreed.

Another knife in the ribs for Novak – beat a slap on the ass by a mile.

One day, I picked up a very old copy of Shakespeare's the Merchant of Venice – and when I say old, I mean *old*! I couldn't believe I understood one word, but I did. I discovered if you read it out loud it helped a lot with the funny language. I loved it - it was so smart. Portia was a clever little minx – she sure sorted that crafty old Jew. Not keen on the love interests though - she deserved better.

I was so busy extolling at the top of my voice, I didn't at first hear a soft laugh. Then, as it became a real chuckle I turned, red-faced at being found out.

I was amazed and embarrassed to see Mrs. Hamilton sitting in the leather chair by the hearth, crystal tumbler poised on its way to her lips.

"Oh, please don't stop. That's the best performance of Shakespeare I've heard since New York. I thought it was a musical when I got the tickets and I never had a better couple of hours sleep in my life."

I picked up again at the bit with Antonio's casket, but the muse had left me, and I apologized.

"Sorry, Mrs. Hamilton. I've never had an audience. I'll work on it."

She put down her glass and took the folio out of my hands, placing it with a thump on the table. She blew a stray lock of hair out of her face.

"Come on," she said. "Let's go and tell that old bastard Novak you were reading Shakespeare, and not climbing-up-the-wall crazy like he told me. I'll enjoy that."

But it was so much better. She fired Jenny who had reported me and threatened Novak that if he didn't quit hounding me, he'd be next. Did he know she'd been at the sauce? Oh, I did hope so!

I discovered I had acquired a new skill. I managed to keep a straight face under the most taxing of circumstances.

As soon as I could, I dashed up to my room and laughed fit to burst, while doing a little jig of pleasure.

There was a multitude of differences between wealthy English people and rich Americans.

In England, people generally inherited their wealth, were pompous and wore funny clothes. Americans on the other hand, were the owners of new money, meaning at most it had come from a grandfather when the continent was first opening up, and hard work brought rewards. The English inherited their wealth over generations, going back in some cases hundreds of years. Half of them were barmy, the others arrogant – some both.

But the American rich looked straight out of Hollywood. Mrs. Hamilton had boxes full of diamond jewelry in a big safe behind some moveable shelves in the library. I don't know why she showed me. She must have sensed I was honest which I absolutely am. I loathe and detest liars and cheats.

She would often drop by the library as I sat quietly reading, and flop into her leather chair with the newspaper, and her habitual decanter - mostly the 'funnies' I guessed, by the expression on her face.

I began to realize over time, she was immensely lonely. She must have been, to choose a parlor maid for company – even one who decimated Shakespeare.

A friendly distance was maintained by tacit agreement. Afterall, she paid my wages, and Addie's too.

Chapter Seven

The Wiz

One summers day, the library windows were propped open, and the scent of roses was carried into the room by a gentle breeze. The books I was reading were beginning to get complicated, so I had taken to making notes on a small pad.

Mrs. Hamilton was sitting by the window. She'd begun to read books as well, mostly Agatha Christie who-done-its. But as usual, I couldn't keep my mouth shut and mind my own business. I pondered, chewing the end of my pencil, and gazing at her head bent over her latest Miss Marple.

"Mrs. Hamilton," I began, tentatively. "Where's Mr. Hamilton?"

This had to be overstepping the mark. I waited for the fallout. She lit a cigarette.

"In jail," she replied as if the question was one she'd expected. "He was caught in '30 running girls for Capone."

Running girls? I'd check that out later. Meanwhile she seemed to have slipped into a revery and flicked her ash into a large urn next to the hearth

"He always was a follower. Never took his own initiative or he wouldn't have ended up working for the mob. You might know his name – Johnny Hamilton. Usually went by the nickname The Wiz because he was good with figures. Which kind, I couldn't say," she added thoughtfully, twisting a stray strand of hair round her finger. She took another mouthful of her drink.

Naturally, I'd never heard of him – nor his boss either. Capone wasn't a common name in Halifax.

This conversation seemed to take the cork from the bottle, and a whole lot more spilled out over a period of time. Pun intended.

After a while she became very frightened by her indiscretion and begged me to keep what she had said to myself.

I promised her faithfully I would and meant it. She nodded with relief. Apparently, without either of us realizing it, we had begun to share confidences like friends. Strange that – the tipsy gangsters moll and the poverty-stricken waif from a foreign land – although 'foreign' is a relative term in America.

Chapter Eight

Love's Labors Lost

I'd forgotten about the letter I'd placed on Addie's bed. She never mentioned it and I never asked.

It came as a surprise therefore, when I saw Alec Maxwell, creeping from apple tree to apple tree around the edge of the library lawn, occasionally ducking behind one of the larger rose bushes if he thought someone was looking. Oh Lord he was so lousy at being clandestine. I was standing in plain sight at the open window, and he was completely oblivious to my presence.

"You can come out now, 'Mighty," I said.

Daddy might be a doctor, but baby son wasn't yet – and at this rate his chances of getting there were pretty slim.

"Come on out, Alec. Your cover's blown," I smiled sardonically, arms crossed.

"I've come to see Addie," he said. *No shit.* "She didn't reply to my letter, and I want to know why."

"Come on. I'll show you how the professionals do it," and so saying, I got hold of him by the sleeve and dragged him round the house to the kitchen door.

When he began to protest at the rough treatment, I put my hand over his mouth and hissed:

"You say one word and I'll gag you."

I pushed him roughly behind the vines of a honeysuckle climbing up the wall by the kitchen door.

"Stay there and keep your trap shut if you want to see Addie this side of paradise."

I was beginning to sound like a gangster's moll myself.

I blatantly walked into the kitchen and asked Mrs. Campbell the cook, if I could speak to my sister for a few minutes in private. I had some family matters to discuss with her.

"Five minutes – no more. She hasn't finished her chores," she said, distracted by her own task.

I grabbed a surprised Addie by the wrist and dragged her outside into the waiting arms of her would-be paramour. She was obviously amazed and her naturally pale skin turned petal pink.

"I'll wait over here and keep watch," I whispered, as I moved out of earshot. "You have five minutes before someone blows your cover. It might be me. I set the whole thing up, so I'd get the blame."

I couldn't hear but I could see Alec pleading his cause, and Addie still pink, swinging coyly from side to side. All she was missing was a floppy hair ribbon and a Teddy bear.

He must have learned something from me as once he had disentangled himself from the honeysuckle, he melted off into the dark kitchen garden, ruining it completely by tripping over and swearing loudly.

That evening as I was wading through a thoroughly soppy poem by Robert Browning, Addie who was sitting on an Ottoman by the window gazing out at the stars, said:

"He wants to take me walking."

"Cheapskate," I said only half aware.

"Do you think I should go? He's a bit…. enthusiastic. It's disconcerting."

"For heaven's sake Addie. If you want to go – go. What's your problem? You've every second Saturday afternoon off."

She looked dubious.

"He has a car. He wants us to go to West Lake - he says it's romantic."

I refused to say any more and on the next Saturday afternoon she zoomed off with Alec in his right-hand drive Morgan. Well, I'd had my chance and blown it. Cool car, though.

Novak was still stalking me, goddamn. What was his problem? I'd paid him back for slapping my derrière. That made us even surely, but apparently I was mistaken.

It seemed I'd put paid to a nice little number he'd got going with Jenny. But the pendulum had swung back the other way, and now I had the upper hand, he had to tread lightly because of the threat of dismissal.

And then, one day, I became a lady's maid and got to call Mrs. Hamilton Marcia. But only in private, of course. In a little over one year, I'd gone from being a bedraggled ragamuffin to confidante of a lady with a dubious past. I was thrilled.

It also meant, with Marcia as sponsor, next year I would be able to apply for my naturalization papers. I'd get those damn papers if it killed me.

Addie, despite her 'beau', wasn't as certain. For the first six months she'd been so homesick she sobbed herself to sleep. It truly was a mystery to me why she'd come. It could only have been because she'd learned to depend on me. The only other option was she missed Halifax, although I would have thought that unlikely.

I saw this as a grand adventure with endless possibilities. She seemed to be terrified by the sheer hugeness of the country. You can walk from Land's End to John O'Groats, across the whole of England and Scotland, without losing sight of human habitation. Often, Lon told me – although I didn't altogether believe him - once outside American city limits, you could travel huge distances without seeing a single soul. She found the prospect terrifying, although she'd never seen anything outside of Connecticut. Which was pathetic.

It wasn't long before hostilities began to loom large on the horizon for the British. It meant my poor English family would have to go through all the trauma again. And of course, there would be casualties.

Within weeks, the Germans were raining bombs down on London, and the major port of Liverpool had been virtually leveled to the ground. My brother Gem had half his face blown away by a hand grenade in Northern France. It was a crushing cruelty he survived.

I was filled with gratitude to a God who had moved me to this wonderful land, and I prayed daily in my heart for those I loved on both sides of the Atlantic.

It came as a surprise when Addie asked Mrs. Hamilton if she could go back to England. I thought she'd have run like a rabbit from the mud, blood and mayhem which was again being inflicted on her country, but she said she couldn't bear the thought of not seeing her brothers again. What had happened to Gem had been the final straw.

I went to see Marcia about her. She must have greased quite a few palms to get her onboard a convoy bound for England. Then that wonderful lady had some special shoes handmade for her with a removable inner lining. Addie was onboard ship before she found the fifty pounds in notes Marcia had secreted there.

Marcia went with me to wave the ship off in New York. She looked more tearful than I did, which said more about me than her I suspected. But then she didn't have to deal with 'Mighty' Maxwell – sister Adelaide left that delight to me.

So I was now alone on the vast continent of America, bursting with excitement and anticipation.

Chapter Nine

'Mighty' and the Lady's Maid

The only places I knew Alec Maxwell from, were a dingy alley off Danbury Main Street, and an unremarkable dancehall in the same town. In the remote possibility I would ever get back to Yorkshire, they'd be scraping my beloved sister off the cobbles of Gibbet Street.

I tried the popular places where young people hung out, but this boy was just not the hanging out type. I doubted he had many friends.

In the end on my next Saturday off, I sought out his parents' home, Annandale. It was set in woodland, isolated by beautiful trees. Wow…it was impressive.

I stood at the end of a long drive, with a gravel turning circle in front of a paneled door. Its brass work, highly polished, gleamed in the bright sunshine. To one side, the approach was lined with lilacs with a scent strong enough to drown out horse manure. Most of the façade of the building was festooned with purple wisteria.

The drive began with two stone pillars with a stag carved on each one. They were overhung by a magnificent European copper beech. Lawns as smooth and even as baize, stretched from one side to the other of the house front.

The blue Morgan convertible Alec had driven Addie in was parked in the drive, together with a Bentley with whitewall tires.

I suddenly realized I'd forgotten to breathe and fell back against the door pillar gasping. How did I tackle this?

I looked down at how I was dressed. I had on a skirt, blouse and a lemon cardigan. Not bad. Thank God I always carried a small mirror, hairbrush and lipstick in my purse. I used the first and second and applied the third, smacking my lips.

Repeating to myself over and over 'I'm as good as they are', even if I wasn't, I pushed up my sleeves, marched the length of the drive and brought down the doorknocker. It was louder than I'd expected.

The door was opened by a replica Jeeves, who looked down his nose at me as if I smelled wrong. He sniffed.

"Yes?"

"I'd like to speak to Alec please."

"*Mr.* Alec," *there was a slight but unmistakable accent on the word Mr.,* "is in the conservatory. If you give me your name, I will enquire if he is available for visitors."

"My name is Grace Harper."

It was all I could do not to add 'what's yours?'

"Very well," and he slammed the door shut in my face.

This was beyond the pale. I pushed my sleeves up further and glowered at the door where his face had been. What was it with the servants in Connecticut? Hadn't they heard of courtesy? He and Novak were cut from the same cloth.

I was so furious, I picked up the doorknocker and gave it another thwack. By this time, my sleeves were pushed up to my armpits. I'd a speech prepared for when he opened the door again which began:

"You jumped-up bast….."

Unfortunately, the door was opened by Alec.

"What're you doing here, Grace? Why the hell are you here?" he said, grabbing my arm.

I shook myself loose. I'd had more than enough for one afternoon. I turned right round and took the road home, all six miles of it, every step fueled by temper. It was a good idea for Addie to go back home - she'd had a lucky escape.

I was hot and sticky by the time I got back to Danbury House. Still furious and still overheated I stripped and took a shower.

"A glass of Glenfiddich would have gone down well!"

I yelled out loud.

As lady's maid to Marcia, the perks were considerable. Firstly, I got my own private room just down the landing from her suite. I also shared her meals which meant coq au vin rather than chicken stew and Duchesse potatoes instead of mash. It didn't appear to me there was much difference.

My room was gorgeous, although I suspect Marcia would have found it very unremarkable. It had chintz curtains in blue and cream with a matching bedspread, and a small armchair by the window, which overlooked a rockery at the side of the house. There was a tall walnut table with curved legs, which held a jug and basin for washing, and a matching chest of drawers and wardrobe which now contained civvies, since I was no longer a house servant.

Since Mrs. Doyle had rightly dumped all our belongings, Marcia had a fine old time helping me pick out stylish outfits, including shoes, a coat with a fitted waist and a mustard jacket. She even bought me a hat a bit like Errol Flynn's in 'Robin Hood'. She showed me how to wear it pulled down over one eye like Marlene Dietrich and gave me some red lipstick so I could be 'en vogue'. I don't know which of us had more fun.

Our final visit was to her beauty parlor where she instructed her stylist how to cut my hair. I'd expected her to suggest her own short, bobbed style, but she didn't. I had long hair which I usually tied in a bun when I was cleaning.

She lit a cigarette, pushed it into an ivory holder and instructed her stylist to cut it just below my shoulders, parted at the side and curled with tongs round the edges like Katharine Hepburn.

In one afternoon, she'd turned me from an ugly duckling into a swan. My wardrobe had a full-length mirror and once alone, I tried everything on and twirled round and round, grinning like an idiot. I looked like a fine lady. In Halifax they'd have said I looked 'fair cracking' – that's if they could summon up the courage to speak to me at all. I had a suspicion I would no longer be welcome in my former home.

Another unforeseen advantage was when Marcia didn't need me, all I had to do was to keep her clothes clean and pressed and tidy her room. As that involved instructing a maid to do the cleaning, it was the stuff of dreams. That maid was always spoken to kindly and received a small tip for her services. Slowly, the news got around and there was competition for the work.

And for having a fine old time Mrs. Hamilton even paid me. I felt as if I'd fallen into a tub of butter.

What's more, I could see the fear in Novak's eyes every time I passed him by. I was now in a position to get back at him and he knew it. Delightful – I'd bide my time and let him sweat a little.

Chapter Ten

Mafia Connections

Despite outstanding business of my own, Marcia decided she needed me to accompany her to Chicago. She'd to get Johnny to sign some papers for the IRS and she was dreading it. I got the feeling she wanted me more for moral support than keeping her clothes in order. She was very tense and took more whisky than usual, so later she'd to lean on my arm as we climbed the airplane steps.

She said she'd rather take the train but flying – first class, of course - was quicker although the worst thing imaginable. She insisted on lending me a fur coat, a pair of earplugs and told me to wear socks. Apparently, it was comfortable but freezing cold and deafening. I wasn't filled with confidence - there seemed something wrong in pretending to be a bird when you weren't one.

We got there safely despite the plane dropping a hundred feet in seconds and scaring me half to death. Marcia said we were lucky it only happened once.

She drank a few more glasses on the flight and ended up sleeping with her head on my shoulder. By the time we arrived in Chicago, I finally understood where the word 'groggy' came from.

We took a cab to The Palmer House hotel on Monroe Street. To get there we'd to cross the whole of downtown Chicago which had much of Halifax about it – soot-blackened buildings, poverty-stricken people.

Unlike Halifax, most folks walked hunched over as if afraid which they probably were. Marcia had told me something about the place. She intended staying as short a time as possible.

I was so overawed by Palmer House I can only recall impressions rather than details. I remember wondering how the hotel managed to exist at all in the middle of so much poverty and fear.

I'd always believed hotel restaurants were for couples or families celebrating, but the clientele here seemed to be mostly groups of middle-aged men, often overweight, with Brylcreamed hair, sharp suits and cufflinks. Perhaps that was how things were in America.

Everything about the hotel, including the lighting, was soft. The table linen and pillows were starched, the silverware was hallmarked and the mirror in my room had electric lights round it. My feet sank into plush fitted carpets and there was an elaborate Persian rug next to the bed. I sat for a full five minutes with my mouth open, until Marcia called me to unpack her clothes.

The following morning, we took a cab to the Cook County Jail, where Johnny was incarcerated. Any tax problems which could make Marcia travel all this way to get papers signed must be serious.
She left me in the car and instructed the cabbie to wait. She wanted to be off as soon as possible.

Marcia wasn't long. It took maybe twenty minutes until I saw her walking down the steps stuffing the paperwork into her bag. As she did so, a man crept from the shadow of the door, grabbed her under the chin, shouted in her face and lifted her clear off her feet. He ripped the bag from her hand and bolted down an alley at the side of the building. I jumped from the car and was kneeling next to her before he'd even got round the corner.

Marcia was laying across the steps sobbing, bruises from his fingers rapidly developing on both cheeks. Her usually immaculate face was smudged with mascara and the glass on her Cartier watch was smashed to pieces. I lifted her onto my lap and rocked her like a baby, until she stopped crying and sat up. The cabbie of course had fled.

"Come on...we need to get you back inside. You can report what's happened and get them to call another cab," I said, trying for some positivity.

"No...NO!" She looked me straight in the eye imploringly. "No, they'll come back for me. They'll have me followed."

I noticed she'd snapped one of her perfect fingernails in the fracas.

I was puzzled. All this over some IRS forms?

"Well, we've got to do something," I said practically. "You can't sit on the steps all day. I need to go inside and ask them to call another cab, or we're stuck here for the night as well."

As her purse had been stolen, she was reduced to wiping her nose on her sleeve, until I fished a handkerchief from my own bag.

Marcia stood hiccoughing and steadied herself against the wall.

"Thank you, Gracie. Thank you for being with me. I have to scarper before they see me, and think I've been grassing on them."

Sometimes our conversations were guesswork for me. I could only gage every other word.

Marcia continued to refuse help from the police.

Eventually, I managed to flag down a stray taxi and load her inside. We went into the hotel at a run and threw our clothes in our bags. While she paid the check at the desk with money she'd deposited in the hotel safe, I put our stuff in the car – she wouldn't go outside alone – and we zoomed off for the airport.

Once in the air, we had a conversation that would make Jimmy Cagney sound like a boy scout.

Johnny had been responsible for running a prostitution racket in the Red-Light area of South Chicago for Capone. When Capone was jailed in 1931, that also marked the end for a lot of his henchmen, Johnny included. He was imprisoned for twenty years. They never convicted Scar Face for his crimes, but Johnny Hamilton was another matter entirely. He couldn't pay off dozens of local politicians and city officials, filthy rich as he was.

But the biggest shock was Marcia who had been so kind to my sister and me. She had been rescued by this hoodlum from one of his dens of iniquity and treated like a princess. No rhyme or reason. He just fell in love with her.

There was no denying Marcia was terrified. When we got back to Danbury, she took a full decanter of Scotch and didn't leave her room for three days. Then it was only for sandwiches and cigarettes.

When she'd pulled herself together, she spilled the rest of the story to me.

The papers Marcia had taken for Johnny's signature were actually deeds to three of the largest brothels in Chicago, made over to him by Capone to avoid arrest for tax evasion. Clearly, that fell flat.

Johnny in his turn, had passed them on to Marcia to avoid the same situation. It was like pass the parcel. The way things were going, the next recipient would probably be me.

Someone didn't want her – or Johnny – to own the bordellos. They must have been confident Al wouldn't make another appearance. I learned later he was crazy from syphilis and had to be sent to some facility in California. Anyway, he was as nutty as a fruitcake by the time he was released. No problem for any adversary – Capone was clearly a spent force.

I didn't suppose Marcia would have been overwhelmed with grief that the documents had gone. She probably had more than enough money to live well for the rest of her life. She let the matter drop. Whether it was from fear of reprisals or that she couldn't care less, I couldn't say.

From that time on, her drinking increased and I found her snorting cocaine a time or two. Over a period of a couple of years she aged ten. Her immaculate dress and makeup were no more. I vowed seriously to myself, no matter what life might throw at me, I would never, never collapse like she did.

She'd lost interest in the house too, and left everything for Mrs. Doyle, Mr. Novak and me to run between us.

Well, Mrs. Doyle and me. Novak disappeared within a few weeks, concerned only for himself as usual.

Then Marcia went missing. Mrs. Doyle and I checked with her family in Washington, but she wasn't there. She hadn't travelled abroad – her passport was in her bureau drawer. If she had close friends I didn't know of them – she had always struck me as being lonely – almost isolated.

I went through her entire suite looking for documents without turning up a single clue. I called her attorney, her beautician and masseurs. No-one had seen her at all. I was frantic. Something was very wrong.

When Marcia's body was discovered in a lake near Milford, I was heartbroken. She had been a true friend but nobody – including me - was greatly surprised at her fate.

There wasn't a mark on her. Most likely she was full of booze and fell in, but we were only employees so were not entitled to further information

Other than telling them she had family in Washington and a hoodlum of a husband in jail in Chicago, there wasn't a lot I could help them with. Clearly, she was living on ill-gotten gains but as it was all in her name and not Johnny's, there wasn't a lot they could do.

It seemed the only person she'd told about her diamonds in the library safe was me. In fact, I seemed to be the only one who knew about the safe at all. I didn't want her jewelry.

I had plenty of savings from my wages to last me a couple of months. That should see me through, but I admit to stealing a diamond clip from her jewelry case as a memento. I didn't think she'd mind.

The rest of the jewels I left. Someone'd get a rare bonus when they came to dismantle the library or demolish the house.

As a final act, I took the Shakespeare folio from the library, slipped it inside a pillowcase from my bed and packed it in the bottom of a suitcase.

Her Will was lodged with the local Probate office and the house put up for sale on the instructions of her attorney. We were given a month's pay and our notice by Mrs. Doyle. Then we had to gather our things and leave. I had a few extra days to pack away Marcia's personal belongings and forward them to Washington, then I had to go too.

I don't know what happened to Mrs. Doyle. She was a lady with much experience of running a household, so I don't suppose she was unemployed for long.

Chapter one of my stay in America was well and truly over. I needed to find a start to chapter two. But I had one more job to do before I left.

.

Chapter Eleven

Cream Tea at Annandale

I had moved into a small apartment with a couple of the other girls from Danbury House. It was depressingly dark, and not very clean but it would do for a couple of weeks until I could decide what to do next.

I donned the very best clothes Marcia had bought me, pulled my one and only hat down over my left eye, blotted my lipstick and took a cab for Annandale.

I rapped on the door and 'Jeeves' opened it, his nose a little lower when he saw this fashionable young lady standing on the doorstep. This time, he invited me into the hall.

"Please tell Mr. Alec, Miss Grace Harper wishes to speak to him." I said, assuming the imperious manner of Marcia's guests to the servants and praying he wouldn't remember my name.

"Mr. Alec is out momentarily but I will fetch Mrs. Maxwell."

This was not going as planned at all.

He showed me into a pleasant little room opening off the hall. Pulling off my kid gloves, I sat down on a button-backed velvet chair, gazing out of the tall window. The leaves of the maples and white oaks on the edge of the surrounding woodland had fallen weeks ago and lay in a brilliant patchwork along the edge of the lawns.

A woman's voice interrupted my thoughts.

"Hello. Miss Harper, isn't it? I'm Mrs. Maxwell, Alec's mother – please do call me Janet. I'm afraid Alec isn't here at the moment, but I'm expecting him back at any time. He's over at Wolcott, clay-pigeon shooting with his father and uncle."

She was so relaxed in her manner she immediately put me at ease. I couldn't imagine anyone being uncomfortable with her.

"While we wait, I would be so pleased if you would join me for tea in the conservatory. Bingley, please take Miss Harper's hat and coat. This way, my dear."

I followed her through her beautiful home, over Persian carpets, and past antique hall furniture. There was a grandfather clock which dolefully chimed the quarter hour, and highly polished golden maple doors with bright brass knobs and key escutcheons. This was old money I realized. Alec's mother was a lady in the old sense of the word.

She was a little overweight, slightly taller than me and wore a heather-colored tweed skirt and violet twinset, and the most beautifully lustrous string of pearls I had ever seen. Incongruously, she had on a pair of house slippers.

The conservatory resembled a large greenhouse with palms, and pots of flowering orchids and gardenias. Very green and white and fresh.

In the center of the room was a circular wrought-iron table covered with a spotless cloth. I was very surprised to see it spread with a typically English cream tea. A cake-stand with French fancies and tiny scones, pots of jam and cream, delicate sandwiches, and a large Minton teapot with matching sugar bowl, cream jug and plates.

She seemed to be entirely alone, so I assume this was how aristocratic ladies spent their afternoons. How would I know?

"Do sit down, dear," and to a hovering maid. "Please fetch a place setting for Miss Harper... and better make some fresh tea."

The maid curtsied and picked up the tea pot. I glanced at her. I'd seen her at the dances at the Starlight Lounge. I sat on crossed fingers, praying she didn't recognize me. She hadn't seemed to.

I copied Mrs. Maxwell's manner at the tea-table. The sticking out of little fingers while taking tea I discovered, was not the usual thing. Marcia had got that wrong – but then Marcia was no lady.

I learned more about social graces in fifteen minutes from Janet Maxwell, than I had learned in my previous eighteen years.

We were just chatting our way amicably through our second cup of tea, when the front door was flung open with a crash violent enough to take it off its hinges.

I heard a shout, and running footsteps, and Alec sweating red-faced and terrified, burst into the conservatory, closely followed by two older tweed-clad gentlemen I took to be his father and uncle.

"Mama, MAMA! The whole of our navy and most of our air force have been destroyed by the Japanese on Hawaii. There are thousands and thousands of American dead." He burst into tears.

Mrs. Maxwell and I both jumped to our feet. She, being more socially adept, managed to deposit her cup on the table. I wasn't and didn't – her beautiful Minton ware was smashed across the conservatory floor.

"Are you sure you're not over-reacting, dear?" said his mother.

Alec straightened his spine in response, blew his nose loudly on a hankie he'd taken from the pocket of his tweed pants, and answered her:

"No Mama. It's true about the attack but I may have exaggerated the number of dead, although I believe the numbers are considerable."

He was almost formal in his speech.

"Sit down son, before you fall down. Dora…" to the hovering maid. "Get us all some hot sweet tea."

The maid curtsied and ran off, no doubt to also relay the news to the other servants.

Mr. Maxwell kissed his wife on the cheek.

"It appears to be entirely correct, Jan. The President has confirmed it on the radio - they are playing it repeatedly with the national anthem. We have been at loggerheads with the Japs for years, but this kind of butchery could never have been anticipated. The number of casualties has not been released, but the entire fleet is gone and much of the air force."

He suddenly seemed to run out of energy and sat down hard on one of the chairs and put his head in his hands.

"Are we in danger of invasion do you suppose Bill?" asked his wife.

She was very pale. Her husband raised his head and shrugged his shoulders.

"Who can say? All I know is I'm glad I don't live in California. They must be terrified."

As an outsider I was becoming increasingly uncomfortable. This family of strangers was shocked to the core. I stood, thanked Mrs. Maxwell for her kindness and asked her to excuse me. Alec looked at me with vague recognition as I passed to collect my hat and coat but said nothing. I don't think the others saw me at all.

Another walk home – and in heels too. I glanced down with resignation at my expensive Ferragamos.

As I skirted the bottom of the drive and stood under the giant beech to pull on my gloves, there was a shout, and Alec came dashing down the drive, long legs pounding.

"Wait. Grace. Let me take you home. Just let me get the car."

The shoes would live to see another day. What a relief.

He opened the door for me and handed me inside as if I was a real lady.

"My mother just gave me a wigging for bad manners. Her stock phrase is 'Remember you're a Maxwell'. In this case she was right. I really am sorry."

How in hell would Addie have coped with someone who'd had a 'wigging for bad manners' from his mother?

We drove to the freeway in silence. The main road traffic seemed very heavy for that time of day.

In order to get back to my apartment, we'd to pass through an estate of large houses with extensive lawns, which were full of people chattering and gesticulating. As far as I could make out owners, servants, gardeners and an assortment of tradesmen were all mixed together. There were people running from one house to the next down the sidewalks and across the road. We nearly collided with several pedestrians who seemed oblivious to our presence.

Alec pulled into the curb.

"This is impossible - I'm going to kill somebody. We'll need to walk the rest of the way – come on."

I nudged him to look away and whipped off my designer shoes and silk stockings - no way was I ruining either – and we set off to walk back to Danbury and my apartment. I figured about five miles – maybe a little less.

The panic seemed to be spreading by the minute. Each communication, whispered or shouted, appeared to be making matters worse. The turmoil increased as we half-ran down the road. Someone shouted to us:

"Did you hear anything else? Jerry here says they're firing on California – Santa Monica I think."

"I shouldn't think that at all likely," said a short-tempered Alec who had nearly fallen over a woman carrying a wailing child.

"Come on," he said to me, took my hand and proceeded as best he could, to jog through the throng.

As we neared the town it was clear things had gotten worse. The whole of the center was jammed by crowds – men women and shrieking children - standing shoulder to shoulder in a state of panic. Alec was beginning to look alarmed himself and stopped to assess the situation.

"Not far… one block down Main Street, then left on Second," I panted, my chest heaving.

By this time, my feet were beginning to bleed and my ankles to give way. I stumbled and gripped Alec's arm to stop myself from falling. He clung to me rather longer than was necessary under the circumstances. I glanced sideways, frowning. He grabbed my hand again and pulled me down the sidewalk skirting the shops, windows for the most part closed and shuttered. We avoided getting dragged into the throng. Suddenly a single voice rang out:

"Quiet! The President's back on the radio!"

A man had dragged a radio set through one of the shop doors, its lead still attached to a plug inside. The silence was instant – you could have heard a pin drop.

A familiar voice boomed out across the street. Unfortunately, we only heard the conclusion of the speech, but it was all we needed.

"......With confidence in our armed forces, with the unbounding determination of our people. we will gain the inevitable triumph so help us God.

I ask that the Congress declare that, since the unprovoked and dastardly attack by Japan on Sunday, December 7, 1941, a state of war has existed between the United States, and the Japanese Empire."

The whole street erupted into cheers and masculine shouts of: "We'll show 'em! We'll get the bastards! We'll teach 'em what it means to mess with America!"

Their women grasped the arms of fathers and brothers, grandfathers and cousins, shouting support and encouragement for their men. Children wailed at the ear-splitting noise.

We pushed through other people, intent on reaching the street and arrived at the doorway to my apartment

And suddenly there was a loud buzzing in my ears and pinpricks of light before my eyes. The last thing I remember were arms catching round my waist before I drifted into oblivion.

I don't think I can have been out very long. Those inconsequential things which always seem to go with regaining consciousness began to surface in my brain – there was a bit of grit stuck in one of the grazes on my foot, my skirt was pulled up at one side.

I looked up to see Alec gazing down at me. Funny, I'd never before noticed how brightly blue his eyes were. Once he saw I was coming to, he struggled with the aid of a lady I'd never seen before, to get me back on my feet. He was scrabbling about in my purse, I assumed for my key.

"Front pocket," I managed to gasp.

How in the hell he managed to get me up the stairs to my first-floor apartment, I will never know. I was gently laid on my bed and the cover pulled over me. I must have slept because when I awoke, the window was open, and the street noise had subsided.

I stared up at motes dancing in a sunbeam above my head. Time to find out what had happened. As I sat, I found I had a partially dried teacloth place across my forehead. I dropped it on the floor as I stood, unsteadily at first.

Alec must have been exhausted. He was sprawled out in my one and only armchair, long legs splayed, chin resting on his chest. I could at least fix him some coffee. He had been my 'knight in shining armor' for a whole afternoon. Hard to think now I had gone to Annandale to yell at him for dishonoring my sister. Damned if addled Addie deserved him!

Once I started clattering in the kitchenette, he soon stretched and rubbed his eyes, turning sleepily round.

"Your color's better," he observed.

"No kiddin'," I replied. And then as it sounded more abrupt than I'd intended, "Thank you for taking care of me."

He chuckled and I handed him his coffee.

"You're learning American English. My mother wouldn't have the faintest idea what you were talking about! She's from Annan in Dumfriesshire – in Scotland," he said. "Oh damn… do you have a telephone? I need to get in touch with her before she calls out the police."

"Not here, but there's a pay booth a block down."

When he came back he said as his mother was in a bit of a state he'd better go home.

"Though if you don't mind just to make sure you're okay, perhaps I could take you for something to eat this evening?"

I was a novice at this, but even I knew you didn't leap at the chance – outwardly anyway. Cool was best - but not cool enough to let the fish off the hook.

"Do you think that would be the right thing to do? I'd hate to collapse on you again," I said acting the ingenue.

57

"How thoughtless of me. Of course you must rest."

To hell with cool.

"I'm sure I'll be fine though if we don't stay out too late. Do you have somewhere in mind? Is there a dress code?" I asked hopefully.

"Not really. There's a lovely little Italian place not far away. Smart casual will do."

He kissed my hand then left. My legs felt oddly wobbly.

It was a lovely evening of pasta and parmesan. A man with oily hair and a moustache played 'O Sole Mio' on a slightly out of tune violin. I confess to being a bit squiffy on red wine by the time we left, which is probably why, when we got back to my door, we ended up in a romantic clinch on the doorstep. We both looked a bit shocked as we drew away, and he said a muffled goodnight.

My God, I must have been one hell of a lousy kisser.

Chapter Twelve

East of the Atlantic

I spent the next weeks reading every newspaper report I could find about the tragedy in Hawaii and its aftermath.

Alec may have been exaggerating the numbers of American dead, but not significantly, as there were well over two thousand. There was also a concerted submarine attack on coastal defenses near Santa Barbara, several weeks after Pearl Harbor in Hawaii.

Of course, there was hysterical fear of renewed hostilities.

Large numbers of enemy planes had attacked Los Angeles. Not true, as it turned out, but an enormous amount of ammunition was blasted into the sky by panicked anti-aircraft crew, before everyone calmed down. Then there were reports of a vast UFO which trawled the California coast before zooming out to sea.

When I hadn't heard from Alec, and these reports had started to get bewildering, I decided to go to Annandale and make enquiries. Surely no-one could object to that. His mother had been agitated too. Perhaps she had been taken ill? The more I considered it, the more concerned I became.

I was also somewhat aggrieved Alec hadn't been back in touch, given our short romantic interlude on my doorstep.

Wearing more sensible shoes, I took a cab to the Maxwell home and hefted the enormous brass doorknocker.

Bingley, who forever in my mind would remain Jeeves, opened the door.

"Good afternoon, Miss. I'm afraid Mr. Alec is not available at the moment. Shall I ask if Mrs. Maxwell is at home to callers?"

I handed him my coat and gloves, then went to the sitting room without being asked. He stuck his toffee-nose in the air again.

When Janet Maxwell greeted me, I was alarmed at her appearance. Naturally, her dress, hair and make-up were impeccable. But her face was drawn and tired.

"Please do come through to my sitting room, Grace dear. Dora…" she called, "tea please…" then turning to me, "or something stronger – sherry or brandy, perhaps?"

This was not looking good. I was starting to feel alarmed – it was only two o'clock in the afternoon. Ladies like Mrs. Maxwell just didn't hit the hard stuff that early. Tea would be fine I told her.

Once we were seated, she took my hand between her own and said:

"Please don't be alarmed Grace, but Alec has volunteered for the Marines. They took him straight away. He left for Boot Camp in San Diego a week ago. I don't know any more because until he completes his basic training, he isn't permitted communications from home."

She stopped and her eyes filled with tears.

"And Bill has been sent to Texas to train medical staff to take care of the wounded."

She couldn't suppress a sob.

Having not the first idea of what to do, I simply hugged her. Apparently, it was the right thing as she put her head down on my shoulder and wept.

The maid Dora came in with the tea. I motioned for her to put the tray down and leave. This was not a weakness Mrs. Maxwell would have liked broadcast to the staff.

When she'd recovered, she pulled out a large man-sized handkerchief she'd had tucked up her sleeve and blew her nose loudly.

"Dear Grace, what on earth must you think of me?"

Think of her? Goddam, the woman had just had her only son and husband whipped away to war. I thought she was a heroine.

"My family lived through a war. If it's any comfort to you, your husband is not on the front line and your son is receiving the best training possible. You and I need to find something practical to do. Any ideas?"

"I'm a reasonable copy typist," she said, which surprised me. "And I learned shorthand as a girl in Scotland. Its beyond rusty, but I'm sure I could pick it up again pretty quickly."

"That's the plan for you. What about me then?"

"Once I find out where Bill is, perhaps I could ask him to get you into training as an auxiliary nurse. I hardly know you but even so I can tell you are intelligent and resourceful."

"Not very sympathetic, though. That can't be good," I said ruefully.

"It might just be to your advantage. I would guess it's sometimes a good quality when dealing with severe wounds."

Both of us burst into tears at that point. This was just ghastly. The war in Britain had faded into the background. It was so far away, so not part of my existence anymore. In any case, Gem was out of it on medical grounds and Robbie and Freddie were still too young.

But this was here, in my adopted and increasingly loved homeland. And a boy I was becoming fond of was training for the front line.

Janet rang round and got a job almost immediately as an air force plotter, tracing the location of our craft in the Pacific and increasingly in the Atlantic, as America committed to supporting our British friends.

As the situation became worse and as more and more of our boys finished their training, there was an increasing stream of troops from all services relocating to the British Isles.

It wasn't quite so straight forward for me. As I didn't fancy banging in rivets – not that the choice was mine - skivvying in a military hospital didn't look so bad. I was hardnosed enough to survive its rigors, and I could write letters home for the boys, like the auxiliaries did in the Great War.

Janet had to call in some favors from colleagues of Dr Maxwell as her husband was in transit for some place abroad. We could only assume the letter informing her of his posting was lost en route as she knew nothing about it. Or perhaps the almighty confusion meant a letter had never been sent at all.

We had to go where we were needed of course. Janet was posted to Lakenheath in England. I was shoved through six months intensive training which was totally inadequate. Then I was sent to be a medical gofer on the Western Front in France which seemed to waver back and forth depending on who had the better guns.

Think Grand Central Station on a colossal scale with mud, blood and explosions, multiply it by a thousand and you still won't have come anywhere near. It was mayhem. Janet and I lost touch pretty much straight away.

My first posting was just to the west of Caen, near the Normandy coast. There weren't many of our boys over yet but we medical staff had been seconded to help with the appalling casualties suffered by the British and Canadians along the Channel coast. My life began anew with my experiences over the next twelve months.

Chapter Thirteen

Mud, Blood and a Fateful Meeting

Eventually, I had to admit to myself that Janet was lost to me for now, at least. There was just no time for anything other than my daily duties.

After three weeks, I was given a uniform two sizes too big but thank God it had trousers and not the stupid white aproned things the first wave of girls had to contend with. Landing on your posterior in a skirt amidst the mud and blood was no fun.

We combat auxiliaries were all in the same boat so terror made us comrades pretty quickly. Talking out the day's traumas was an unbelievable relief. Just to cry with someone who knew what you were going through eased the burden.

Not too often at first, the Krauts struck lucky, and we ended up with tents full of wounded. Our unit was mostly involved in triage, which sometimes amounted to figuring out which young boy was going to die first.

It was organized chaos. The qualified nurses were so stretched, because they were taking the load off the few doctors by diagnosing the injured and instructing us. We learned to stitch, disinfect, dress wounds, hold sick buckets, mop brows, set up drips – all the time smiling cheerfully and telling some eighteen-year-old with his leg hanging off from the knee, that he'd be patched up and on leave before he knew it.

After a few weeks we were moved to another facility where the fighting was particularly fierce on the eastern suburbs of Caen.

It's not a rare story for the times, but occasionally, all we could do was mop brows, and sing a few lines about bluebirds over Dover. That always seemed to cheer them up, as it had been some time since anyone had seen a bluebird over Dover. As far as I knew, Dover had yet to see a goddam bluebird as they all lived in America. Still, it seemed to be a source of hope when other things failed.

The gloriously green and lush French countryside, with its quaint little old-fashioned villages and beautiful medieval churches, was being reduced to rubble by soulless hooligans in uniform.

So, circumstance had taken me from Yorkshire to Connecticut them back across the pond in five years. I had reached my majority and still didn't have those damn papers, even though there was every chance parts of me might be decorating the French landscape on America's behalf in the very near future. Surviving wasn't an option – it was an obligation.

Last I'd heard, Alec was at Boot Camp near San Diego, on the other side of the world. I'd heard nothing of him since, so there was probably no point in looking for him. He could literally be anywhere on earth. In fact, the entire Maxwell family was an unknown.

When and if this damn conflagration ever finished, where would I go? I'd no real home anywhere. Marcia was dead and her employees scattered; for all I knew Janet, Bill and Alec were debilitated or deceased. So, I'd to think where I wanted to go and what I wanted to do. I was only twenty-one and this couldn't go on forever. Someone, for better or worse, would have to run out of money. And no way on God's earth was I going back to England.

Late one afternoon, when I'd managed to snatch time to myself, I climbed the steep spiral stairway to the top of the massive walls of Caen Castle and sat on the parapet overlooking the neatly painted buildings of the old town. The people skittered about like ants on the cobbled streets far below, chasing this way and that, their clamor deadened by distance. I turned my sweating face to the cool breeze. Bliss.

I scrabbled in my pocket for my cigarettes, shook one out and reached for my lighter. It would be such a delight to sit peaceful and undisturbed, for just a little while.

A hand reached out, took the cigarette from my mouth and a man, shading the flame against the breeze, lit my cigarette, and one of his own. I'd seen him before. He was one of the junior doctors from my unit, but I didn't know his name.

I frowned, annoyed at having my solitude disturbed.

"Hope you don't mind," he said with a lopsided grin, wriggling his butt to make way for it on the wall. "I saw you climb up here and thought you might like some company."

How wrong can you be!

He had that unique Gallic manner which implied 'you are the only being in creation I could ever hope to love', at the same time sucking in the smoke from his first Gauloise of the day and twisting the stem of his glass of vin rouge.

He stuck out his hand and said:

"I'm Charles Riviere de Beauvais – Charlie Rivers to you," again that smile as he raised my fingers to his lips. I changed the gesture to a handshake.

"Charlie Rivers? Give me a break!" He ignored me by speaking over the top.

"So, you're the beautiful Grace, who has all the boys below in a spin."

I curled my lip in distain.

"Very funny. Sarcasm is the lowest form of wit," I snarled, "Go annoy someone else. This castle wall's taken."

I blew away a stray lock of hair which had stuck against my forehead.

'A long way from Katharine Hepburn.' I thought wryly. 'Marcia would be mortified.'

"Ah....," he insisted, "...but the highest form of intelligence."

He seemed to have an answer for everything. As if he'd read my mind he said, holding up his hand:

"You might as well give up. Resistance is futile!"

Words like intelligence and resistance were said with a charming lilt.

"What do you want, anyway?" I asked, still not entirely giving up the semblance of irritation. "You can't have climbed all the way up here to tell me I'm destined for Hollywood. What's your angle?"

"Dinner, darling Grace...dinner. You and me." For a minute I was speechless. Here was I looking like Sweeny Todd after my day battling death, and he wanted to take me to dinner.

"Yes. I've actually found a little restaurant near *les Jardins d'Abbaye*. Personally, I think they go out hunting rabbits and call them veal, but beggars can't be choosers!"

He was so appallingly upbeat, I couldn't stay annoyed.

"It'll take too long – I've to be back on night shift at nine," I said, stretching a point. "I'm not biking that far for a plate of rabbit stew."

"Then I shall have to bring my carriage to escort mam'selle. We're both off at seven – that's if the – how you say? - Krauts give us a break. Formal dress optional."

This last echoed back up the steps he was halfway down.

I felt as if I'd just been flattened by a whirlwind. Nevertheless, I hummed riding my bike back to hell-on-earth.

I saw him charging from bed to bed across the next ward tent to mine as I passed. He looked energetic even surrounded by carnage. He was singing 'Pennsylvania Six Five Thousand' at the top of his voice.

Formal dress had to be a joke. I'd to borrow a pair of matching ankle socks – grey rather than white – and the only skirt I had, had a small hole at the waist. I patched it as best I could and ran an iron over it. My only footwear apart from my ward lace-ups which were nasty, were a pair of tennis shoes I'd optimistically included in my kit. I gave them a rub with toothpaste to brighten them up.

God, I felt awful. That bastard would probably turn up in a tux.

But he didn't. He had on a pair of slacks and a cotton shirt and was lounging against an 'acquired' Jeep as I walked up. He wolf-whistled. Now that was cruel.

He threw his arm around my shoulders and, as he handed me into the Jeep for all the world as if it was a Rolls Royce, he bent and kissed me lingeringly on the lips. We were instantly surrounded by wolf-whistles.

My recollection is that he sang Glen Miller tunes with a French accent through all the meandering back streets to the Abbey gardens.

The rabbit turned out to be paper-thin slices of roast beef with a few vegetables I would guess the restaurant owner had grown in his back yard. It was almost like being human again.

Charlie kept up a steady stream of conversation, firing the occasional question my way. I learned he was from somewhere near Deauville – currently pretty much flattened - and his Dad was some kind of civil servant in Paris.

I told him I was English not American – he kissed my hand. I also said my Dad was on the board of a woolen mill, whereas he was actually an overlooker, with one debilitated war veteran son to care for, a couple of girls – one of whom, Addie, was next to useless – and two lads too young for useful work. But that was in England, so he'd probably never find out.

Charlie was so easy to talk to, I eventually ended up telling him the parts of my story I could be truthful about. I even told him about the naturalization papers I hoped to get some day.

"Why don't you have them already? Is there something wrong with you?" he asked guilelessly.

I explained I hadn't been there long enough before the mud and the blood started flying in Europe, but said I intended applying for them as soon as humanly possible.

It was a very pleasant evening but the following day, we were once more ankle-deep. In fact, I didn't see him except remotely, for almost ten days. Then he was sitting on a folding chair puffing away at a cigarette and swinging his foot as if he hadn't a care in the world. He waved cheerfully as I walked by on my way to swill out a couple of bedpans.

A week later, he put his head round our tent flap and asked if I fancied a beer. Just the sight of him made me want to laugh. I'd a couple of hours due so I put my undies to soak and skipped off after him. He took my hand and twirled me round and round until I was dizzy and fell against him, laughing.

La Manche sunsets are tranquil, misty and gentle. The globe of the sun more silver than gold, appears to hover in the air before slowly fading into the liquid sea. I kicked off my canvas shoes and splashed in the shallow water, thrilled for once to be young and free, even if it was for just a little while.

Despite his light-hearted gallantry, Charlie became suddenly serious. It was pure foolishness to begin attachments when the times were so uncertain. Who knew what we might be doing next week or the week after? If we were there to do anything at all. I found myself sobbing into his shoulder.

"Come on, ma Grace. *C'est l'heure de partir*," he said, momentarily subdued.

But you couldn't keep Charlie Rivers down for long. He was soon twirling me through the shallows of the Channel beaches again.

Chapter Fourteen

One Man and his Dog

Alec Alone.

Oh man, Boot Camp was tough. Designed to break a guy and rebuild him from the ground up. Designed to make him forget his former life and live in the present with no thought for the future.

Up at five, five mile run and shower; huge, heavy cooked breakfast – you sure needed that. Then an hour to prepare for inspection, while you prayed the sergeant would miss you and pass on to the next guy in line.

Some of the men made their beds the night before and slept on the floor to make extra time.

Then training, training, training. Running, climbing, jumping, crawling until a guy could hardly stand. A lot didn't make it. The Marines were an elite force, and the fitness requirements were unbelievably tough. That I got through was a miracle.

I hadn't thought much of home. Too busy and too much a subject of military brainwashing, I guess.

I had a whole two weeks leave before I shipped out on my first assignment. I wouldn't know where that would be until I reported back. I sure needed the break. But when I arrived back in Annandale it was to find the house empty. Mom and Dad were both attached to the forces in Europe.

I thought of Grace. Little Grace with the heart and soul of a spitfire. She wouldn't have been at Annandale. In fact,

I had absolutely no clue where to start looking for her. One thing was clear. I had to find her. She had become important to me in a way Adelaide never was.

Sweet gentle insubstantial Addie. She didn't belong in this world of flying explosions and horrible death. She was far too vulnerable, too tender-hearted. I could never have been strong enough for her. I knew she was far from London, which was taking a frightful hammering by German bombers, but nothing else. I just hoped she was far away and those she loved were safe.

Grace was not so beautiful, not so kind and understanding but she had a toughness of spirit which would get us all through this horror.

I tried to ignore the little voice which whispered: 'But what if Grace isn't tough *enough*? What if she bows and snaps under the terrible weigh forced on her by circumstance? I had to believe that wouldn't happen.

The months of training passed in a blur of orders. I'd swapped Boot Camp in San Diego for, finally, the Marine Medical facility in San Antonio. It wasn't the way I'd intended to begin my career, but it seemed at least possible I might be of use helping boys with the most appalling injuries, cope with their shattered lives. The one or two doctors specializing in non-invasive care were considered oddballs but I lapped up what they had to teach.

It was a difficult concept to grasp. How and why did physical problems translate into mental disturbances? In the end it was a moot point - if a young man is decimated in a hail of bullets it's not possible to convince him things will improve. He wouldn't care – he'd just want out.

My mother would have been delighted as it meant I was home-based and wouldn't see active service, but I felt oddly deflated as if I was somehow letting down those I most wanted to help.

It was true, in wartime you have to go where you're most needed and I was required to fix minds not bodies, at least for the time being.

Eventually at the end of my first week of leave, when the sound of gunshot had faded from my ears, I sat down with what seemed like a mile-high pile of mail which had accumulated in my parents' absence. Most of it was rubbish mixed with the occasional account. But amongst the detritus, much to my surprise was a large brown envelope addressed to…Grace.

Not knowing where she was and if the letter was urgent, I sliced it open with my pocketknife.

Inside were some documents, an envelope secured with sealing wax, and a covering letter asking her to contact the administrative offices of Fairfield County, Connecticut. Very strange. She must have left our address for contacting her.

I put the letter to one side. I'd telephone them before I left.

I'd just a couple of days left to myself, so I decided to take Dad's gun up to the clay-pigeon range like in the old days. I didn't know if it was still open, but I'd enjoy the drive and a stroll through the woods in the fresh air in any case.

The incongruities of my life at present were disturbing. One day I was terrified of what my future held, the next I was strolling through fragrant woods in Connecticut where the only noise was the crunch of leaves underfoot.

I breathed in the crisp air and shifted the shotgun further onto my shoulder.

The range was shut and completely deserted. I managed to push my way through a hole in the wire fence. Where once had been pristine footpaths and scrubbed traps, couch grass had poked its way against fence posts and through the gravel. There was a coke bottle propped against one of the wood pilings and screwed-up candy papers nearby.

I felt despondent. It was as if the whole of the world was encapsulated in this one place. What had been clean and cared-for was now scruffy and unkempt. Like my country – like my mother's, and Grace and Addie's homeland. The places that had once been such a proud display of the ingenuity of God – the Louvre, St Paul's Cathedral, Montecasino and so, so many more, had become the playthings of the Devil.

I suddenly felt so alone.

The sun went behind the clouds and the wind became biting. I didn't want to stay here. There was a bad feeling about the place.

As I straightened from returning through the fence I was startled by a low snarl, and I stood to see a tall man in tattered clothing standing between me and the woods. Round his wrist was wound a leather strap. The dog attached to its other end was a horror. It looked to be some kind of pit-bull cross. Its jowls were retracted in a growl and displayed white teeth dripping with saliva. It was straining at the leash and the man was leaning sideways to keep his balance.

My inclination was to run, but the dog would hunt me down in seconds. I straightened my back. Afterall, I was a Marine although yet to prove it.

"What do you want?.," I demanded with more bravado than I felt. The dog renewed its efforts to get free.

"Ich brauche Nahrung für mich und den Hund. Wir hungern" he shouted, obviously trying to convey his meaning by the loudness of his voice, as I clearly hadn't understood a word.

He rubbed his stomach and pointed down his throat, then at the dog which clearly had decided where its next meal was coming from.

"Oh.... you're hungry," I said unnecessarily.

"*Ya...*," he retorted, "*Yaa.*"

In an instant he went from looking aggressive to pathetic. His shirt was ripped in several places. He was grimy and had several days growth of beard. Not wishing to take on the dog, I mouthed, miming frantically:

"*Kommen sie hier,*" which was about all the German I knew, and that came from the newspaper 'funnies'.

I pointed repeatedly towards our house. The President had joined with Mr. Churchill in the British hostilities against the Germans, but I didn't feel particularly threatened. This man was more pathetic than dangerous I felt. Barring the dog that was.

When we got back to Annandale, I nervously instructed him to tie the dog up in the yard out back and led him into the house.

I gave him a hunk of bread and some cheese as he was clearly starving and set about frying some ham and eggs and making coffee.

He startled me by snatching a piece of the meat from my hand and pointed to the door. It clearly was for the dog. I gave him another slice and he bowed his head in thanks.

He looked absolutely shattered. In all honor, I needed to learn this man's situation.

I could see no solution to our dilemma without involving someone else. I didn't speak German and his English was limited. We were both coming to the end of our imaginations as far as mime was concerned.

He'd reached the same conclusion and buried his head in his hands.

"Come," I said. And gave him what he needed to clean himself up. He smiled his gratitude.

But when I offered to find someone to help us communicate, he became very threatening and dragged the dog in from outside.

An hour later we were still sitting at the kitchen table, unable to sort out what to do next.

In the end, he leapt to his feet dragging the dog, and ran as fast as he could through the trees at the far side of the lawn. I let him go. There seemed little point in doing anything else.

As an enemy alien – possibly an escapee from the camp at Windsor - I would be obliged to report him to the authorities. Man's inhumanity to man. He had intended no harm.

It was getting dark, and I was tired. The morning would be time enough to consider my two major problems: how to find Grace and how to report an enemy alien. Life was never simple. When I'd sorted these problems I'd possibly be posted to the front.

Chapter Fifteen

Slaughter at the World's End

Charlie turned out to be something of a surprise.

I'd lied through my teeth about my family circumstances, but then so had he.

Whereas my inoffensive weaver of a Dad had turned into a textile tycoon, the parent of Charlie Rivers was, in truth, a Duke with his own castle and a business empire in Paris.

Of course, this golden nugget of information didn't come from Charlie. I doubt it had even registered his Dad was an aristocrat in a land which had chopped off the heads of its Royalty a hundred and fifty years before.

It came from one of the GIs in a fit of pique. Seems Charlie hadn't been far off the mark when he'd said I had a following.

I don't know what the guy was trying to prove, but it'd take more than a member of a defunct aristocracy to faze Gracie Harper. If Charlie could ignore it, why not me? He'd still be as daft if his name was Roosevelt.

In between bouts of sewing back limbs, swabbing blood-soaked floors and wafting away ever-present flies, the other auxiliaries and I were engaged in boiling dressings in large copper caldrons. It was hot, sweaty work.

One of the hardest things to take in our situation was the constant rollercoaster of emotions. Down in the depths of despair sitting with a young boy as he died, then floating on air when my romantic Frenchman appeared. Then back down to earth.

It takes more than some inconvenient little war, I learned, to separate a Frenchman from his cuisine. He was forever turning up with a cheese in one pocket and chunks of baguette in the other. On one memorable occasion he even managed to smuggle in a bottle of Calvados.

It also didn't take him long to prove you can't separate a Frenchman from his other major pastime.

On our second or third date, Charlie arrived whistling cheerily and swinging a beribboned box.

"*Un petit cadeau pour la jolie m'amselle.*"

I blushed which was stupid as I wasn't altogether certain what a *cadeau* was.

The little velvet box turned out to contain a bracelet with two charms attached. One was an American eagle with rather odd ruby eyes, and the other a fleur de lis of France, set with sapphires. It was truly the most beautiful thing. He must have had it made – somewhere - unless they'd a factory churning them out with a view to *entente cordiale* of a most particular kind. I didn't have the heart to remind him, as yet I was English.

As he latched the bracelet around my wrist, he leaned over and gave me a kiss so gentle it was like a breath of air. I was so entranced I kissed him back.

To this day, the bracelet is kept in a special carved ivory box at the back of my lingerie drawer. It was a treasured secret shared only with a man I once loved so dearly.

The strolls down the leafy flower-bedecked lanes of Normandy took on a more romantic ambience after that.

As I gazed into eyes of hazel green, tender with love, the war seemed a million miles away and, in place of mortar bombs and gunfire, the air seemed filled with bird song.

"Je t'aime ma chère. Tu me possèdes, cœur et âme," he would whisper as he kissed me passionately and stroked my body into ecstasy.

I knew what the first sentence meant of course, but only learned of the second when it was too late.

These moments were precious few. The rest of our time was spent in canvas wards of human carnage.

Yet Charlie – somehow – seemed able to keep his balance, and to drag me along with him. It must have cost him dearly.

His parents' home in Deauville was rubble and Paris unattainable, unless you were a high-ranking officer with connections. Then it was pâté de foie gras and Champagne all the way – at least for the time being.

So, we would fish in a little river close to a village with winding cobbled streets. We cooked the few fish which didn't get away, over wood fires on its banks. On the one night in fourteen when with luck we had a little free time together, we would sleep under the summer stars and Charlie fondly bound my wrists with daisy-chains. Then I would borrow his pocketknife to try and pare out the blood from beneath my nails.

The fighting was becoming more intense, so our country walks had to stop. The allied troops were not doing well, and an increasing number of them were ending up under our care. We were having to move our operation quite frequently which meant transporting the injured as well as our equipment. We'd to pack up and haul the tents through cloying mud, and fields of shattered homes where children's toys mixed with kitchen detritus and filth. After a while, the pounding of guns and boom of flying earth became background noise.

Sometimes my hands were shaking so badly I could hardly attach the drips, and twice I slipped and fell on the wooden planks which served as flooring. The second time, I sprained my wrist and was useless for a day or two. But I couldn't leave – I just couldn't. So, I read to the boys when I could, or wrote letters to mothers or girls at home. Sometimes all they wanted was to hold my hand.

I was glad to be active again when my wrist had healed. These boys were injured, some fatally, and my heart ached for them.

I saw Charlie once or twice from a distance, but we were too busy to speak. He looked haggard which was a measure of the seriousness of his situation. Charlie Rivers was never distressed – he could always find a silver lining.

Then one day when I had worked forty-eight hours at a stretch, I just couldn't do it anymore. I was shaking from head to foot with exhaustion and my speech became incoherent. Dizzy, I fell to my knees, sliding down against the canvas wall.

I worked with professionals. They swung me onto a stretcher and carried it to a small slope under a hedge, one of the few spots with no mud. There they left me.

I must have slept for a while and when I awoke, it was to see my loving Charlie, kissing my hand and holding it to his cheek, with tears running down his face.

"*Oh ma chérie, Oh ma pauvre chérie,*" he repeated over and over again.

I wiped his tears away with my thumb and pulled his head down to kiss him. I guess the whole thing caught up with him at once because he suddenly shook with grief. *Pauvre chérie* indeed.

But he only had a few moments before the panic began again. His name was called urgently. He kissed me quickly on the fingers and lips and fled back to work.

A shell streaked - with a whine and a blast – straight through both hospital units and blew the whole lot – patients, doctors, nurses, tents, bedpans, beds, equipment – high into the smoke-filled air. I saw bits of bodies clunk down in the mud, mixed with the detritus of war. In one place a girl I had been working with twenty minutes before, lay in the mud, unmarked but for the tent post sticking out of her chest. There was an earth-stopping silence.

Chapter Sixteen

A Struggle towards the Light

I had lost six weeks of my life in as many seconds.

I had vague recollections, more snap shots really, shifting and disjointed. If I tried to focus on them, they became dreamlike and faded away. Nothing moved at the right speed.

There was a large sheet of metal stuck through a canvas wall. Oddly unreal, a human eye laid on a clump of grass – I remembered its color distinctly. It was hazel green. A nurses' watch stuck at 4.22, its glass shattered. A bank of dog daisies splashed with red. In all my dreams the whole dislocated mess was covered with viscus, cloying mud. There was no human voice, but I couldn't tell if there was no-one there or I was deaf. Then I was gently lifted, and I seemed to hear a far distant scream.

It could have been six minutes, it could have been six years. I had no way of knowing - time had ceased to be a reality. But slowly my surroundings began to coalesce.

The first sensation I was aware of was the cool fresh feel of starched linen. It smelled heavenly. I lifted one hand. It felt odd, as if it didn't belong to me. It was clean, but that had to be wrong.

For a long time, I lay still, trying to make sense of my surroundings. What did I know? It was silent so either I was deaf, or I was alone. I didn't seem to be deaf because I could hear my hand move on the sheet. Alone, then.

The past blasted back at me with the force of the shell which had ended my lover's life. I screamed and screamed. I couldn't draw breath and started to choke. I spluttered then my body of its own volition screamed again.

There was a pounding of feet, and the door was flung open. Like the door when I'd first heard the news of war. War? Then the real pain started. I began to remember.

My thoughts must have shown clearly on my face because someone took my hand and gently pushed me back against the pillow.

"Charlie!," I gasped. "Fetch Charlie. I want to see him." But I already knew it was pointless. The last time I'd seen him he was strewn in pieces across a field in France.

I felt the sting of a needle in my arm.

When I came to again, I was looking into startlingly blue eyes. I knew them. Where did I know them from? His face came into focus. It was Alec Maxwell….'Mighty' Maxwell. How unbelievably strange. He wasn't in France. Was he? I tried to sit, and he pushed me back again. I could see a nurse hovering behind his right shoulder. She was bathed in sunlight like an angel.

"More amytal. Sufficient to calm her, that's all."

When I stood outside myself, I knew this was the right thing to do, but I still struggled as the nurse adjusted the drip.

"Lie still, Grace," Alec instructed. He sounded so authoritative I obeyed at once. He sent the nurse away so we could speak in private.

"Gracie... there's no need for you to tell me anything now unless you want to. I know the bare bones of what happened. You can fill in the details later."

I drew a deep breath and felt it rattle down my grazed throat:

"Alec...." I reached for his hand and actually said, "Where am I?"

"You're in the Mallinson General Hospital psychiatric unit in New York."

I tried to sit up in bed again. I was truly panicked. I instantly started to react, shocked awake by his last statement.

"No... Alec. Don't let them. Don't let them take my brain away. Please."

"I promise you faithfully there will be no lobotomy. This is an experimental facility. We're trying to develop a way to treat battle fatigue by other means... sedatives – like the sodium amytal the nurse has just given you. Then perhaps hypnosis coupled with massage. All this is to induce a calmness which will allow you to rediscover and deal with your trauma."

How could I ever.... ever recover from the horror of seeing my love lying in pieces in the mud. I said:

"I can't recover, Alec. Never, from what I saw."

I looked at him imploringly and he leaned over and kissed my forehead.

"I promise you will at least get your life back, Gracie. I promise you that, whatever it takes."

And he was right. When the hospital had done what they could for me, I was sent to a rehabilitation center in the peace of the Litchfield Hills of Connecticut until I was fit to go home.

There was only one problem with that. I didn't *have* a home. The outbreak of war caught me between Marcia Hamilton's house and a rented apartment in Danbury.

I could do no other than to ask for Alec's help, so I called him at work in New York.

His reaction was instantaneous. I should stop at Annandale. It had been empty for a while and I'd be doing him a favor. He'd ring the staff immediately. Going from no home to a mansion was disconcerting to say the least.

"By the way, there's an envelope addressed to you in the bureau in dad's study. It came a couple of years ago, but I didn't know how to reach you," said Alec.

Who on earth would write to me? Who could? The mail from England was heavily censored if it got here at all. Anyway, apart from me, of my family only my sister Addie had been able to read and write but I didn't suppose it could be from her.

Marcia was dead. It might have been from Mrs. Doyle or Novak. Decidedly unlikely. Who then?

Chapter Seventeen

Marcia's Bewildering Bequest

Alec had some leave coming so when I was discharged, he picked me up and took me home with him. I was so unbelievably grateful. This was kindness I'd never known.

When we arrived at Annandale, he settled me in, then fetched the package from his father's study. He had Dora fetch coffee to the dining room and we examined the contents together.

It turned out to be a copy of Marcia's Will.

"Oh, what a great surprise," I said. "A few bucks will ease matters considerably. Might even be able to rent a place of my own."

There was a covering letter explaining that the Will couldn't be executed until the whole house had been cleared and giving a number for a firm of attorneys in Danbury.

The first page was the usual 'sound of mind' stuff. It was clearly written some months before when she still was – of sound mind, that is.

Page two got down to the detail. Alec ran a finger down the entries until he found my name, then sat down looking puzzled. Wow! That was worrying. He redirected my attention to the page before me which read:

"*Danbury House and all its contents are to be sold. Half of the money goes to my husband, John William Hamilton on his release from whichever jail he finds himself in at that moment, on condition he stay out of trouble for one year. If he should fail to do this, the money is to be donated instead to the High Watch Recovery Centre, Alcohol Abuse Unit, Kent, Connecticut, to use at their discretion."*

I was confused. What had this to do with me? Alec told me to read on.

"The only exception to the sale is the contents of the library entire, which I leave to my friend Grace Harper, in thanks for the happy hours we spent there together. I have attached to this Will and Testament a sealed letter for her private attention."

Puzzling indeed!

I told Alec about the beautiful leather-bound volumes I'd discovered there. He was impressed and thought they might be worth quite a bit more than a few dollars.

The rest of her estate went to a sister in Washington DC and her children, and $500 to Mrs. Doyle with thanks for her loyal service.

Then there was a whole page of instructions on administration, and a disclaimer which read:

"If this Will, in part or in its entirety should be challenged at any time by any of the legatees, or if its terms or conditions are disputed, that petitioner shall have their bequest revoked and the money donated to the said High Watch Recovery Centre."

Alec handed me the letter clipped to the back of the Will, yellowed but still bearing its wax seal intact.

"This will just be an explanation of why she did what she did, I expect. Marcia's death was desperately sad. To me and Addie she was always so kind.

"Do you mind if I take it to my room to read alone?" I asked.

He smiled and held out my chair.

On the bed, I broke the seal on the envelope. Then sat back, baffled.

"W24-E59-W76 – take a big bag."

There was also a key, which I recognized was for the French windows into the library at the side of Danbury House.

I turned the document over in case there were any further instructions on the back. Marsha clearly thought it should be something I would understand. I shook my head - no idea.

I loved the thought of the books though. There was no way I would let them go.

I asked Alec if there was anywhere I could store them temporarily at Annandale, and perhaps his father could use some of the bookshelves? Anything not required, Alec said he would make arrangements to sell at auction, but he'd have to do it from New York, as he'd to report back to the hospital in a couple of days. The books could be piled up in one of the guest rooms. He didn't think his mother would mind.

I saw him off a couple of days later. He hugged me more lingeringly than might have been appropriate, but then he was inclined to be emotional.

As he drove away, I turned to go back into the house when like a bolt from the blue, it suddenly struck me what the number was.

I ran back inside, grabbed the contents of the letter, called a cab and hightailed it to Danbury House.

I'm absolutely positive Marcia had planned this to resemble one of the Agatha Christie novels she so loved, so I played along.

I crept up the side of the house like a veritable Miss Marple, through overgrown flowerbeds, and profuse honeysuckle growing over the kitchen door, and entered the library.

I pushed back the secret shelves and dialed what I had taken to be the combination to the safe. It clicked almost musically.

Her boxes of jewels were stacked neatly inside, most in velvet boxes – a few in abalone or cloisonné cases. I opened the top one just to check I'd got it right. There might even be enough to buy a nice apartment and furnish it as well.

Things like this just didn't happen to the likes of Gracie Harper, so I stamped hard on my excitement.

I closed and relocked the safe and moved the shelves back into place. This would need more thought - Marcia had clearly not given it her full attention. If I was caught taking the jewels from the library secretly, it might be thought I was stealing them. I'd empty the books first, then go and see Marcia's attorney, show him the letter and explain.

Mr. Moffat of Moffat, Moffat and Linden reread the Will and carefully appraised Marcia's letter. He couldn't think there was a problem but would take a copy to check with a colleague just to be on the safe side. His fellow attorney could find no loopholes either.

The following day, I met Mr. Moffat outside Danbury House and will him was a man he introduced – fittingly - as Mr. Price, who he said would be able to tell me which items of jewelry were genuine, and which paste. In the unlikely event there were a few real pieces amongst them, he should be able to tell their approximate value. Mr. Price had brought along his little glass microscope-thing and waved it under my nose like some badge of office.

In the library, he tiptoed to the window checking it was locked, looked carefully outside and pulled shut the drapes.

"Can't be too careful," he said in a posh accent as if he'd been to Harvard. Not likely I thought, looking at the rest of him.

I opened the safe and still tiptoeing, he carefully arranged the contents on the library table.

It was the oddest thing. I suddenly felt as if Charlie was standing just behind my left shoulder. The feeling was so strong I turned around. Nobody there of course but the feeling persisted. I was overcome with a crushing sadness and was obliged to sit down in Marcia's chair.

Mr. Moffat thought I was overcome by the sight of my riches and offered to fetch me a glass of water from the kitchen, for which I thanked him but refused.

Meanwhile, Mr. Price was peering at a necklace through his glass and sweating. He kept glancing my way and making pencil notes on a pad.

He'd sorted the boxes to his left and right. One, that on the right, was considerably bigger than the other which comprised three largish items. Three out of fifteen boxes wasn't bad, I mused. I'd seen Marcia wear her jewelry.

That had to be the cheap stuff in the other pile. There was plenty of it.

Finally, Mr. Price concluded his appraisal and stood grimly before me, swinging pompously up and down on the balls of his feet.

"Well, Miss Harper. I should congratulate you. You've a nice little bequest here…yes, very nice indeed."

He reached across and took the top box of the pile of three and opened it. It was one of Marcia's favorites – I'd seen her wear it often. It was diamonds with a ruby teardrop pendant.

"This, I'm afraid, is quite definitely paste. Would you like to see through my glass?"

As it would mean not a thing, I declined.

"And these other two the same."

Mr. Moffat gave an impatient cough. Mr. Price looked irritated.

"These, however, are all the real McCoy."

He began to open the boxes and lay them out one by one on the tabletop. There were individual items of earrings, necklaces and bracelets. The most spectacular items though, were suites.

One was a necklace, bracelet and earrings of white gold spangled with hundreds of tiny diamonds which caught the light and shimmered and sparkled, almost like dewdrops on a spider's web.

The other had an enormous deep purple tanzanite centerpiece flanked by diamonds. It was so big as to be almost a pectoral. It was horrible.

I looked from Mr. Moffat to Mr. Price and back again, eyes popping out of my head.

"How much?" I finally managed to get out.

"Well, I can't be absolutely certain of course, but I would say upwards of fifty million dollars."

I must have gone ashen – I certainly felt dizzy – because Mr. Moffat poured me a large brandy from Marcia's ever-present stock on the corner bar. I noticed he poured himself one too.

"With your agreement, Miss Harper," Mr. Price intoned, "I will arrange for these to be deposited with a bank. Do you have a preference?"

I shook my head, still stunned.

"Then if you will leave it in my hands. Mr. Moffat and I will issue an inventory, then you can check everything before it's moved."

Chapter Eighteen

A Secret, A German and the Return of a Lost Friend

I wish I could say I felt like a wealthy woman but in truth I would have given the whole lot to get Charlie back. What was money when there was such a hole in my heart?

Always in my mind was a picture of his face, tender and so obviously French with its smooth olive skin, and the mischievous sparkle in his hazel-green eyes meant just for me. I cursed God for taking him from me when we'd just found each other. I may be as rich as Croesus, but without Charles Riviere de Beauvais my life was empty and over, its course run.

Never the easiest person to get on with, I now started snapping at people for no reason at all. I discovered a cruel streak in my nature I never knew I had.

The only person safe from my tongue lashings seemed to be Alec. How could I be like that with a man who had helped me in any way he could? I once called him son-of-a-bitch and such was his distress, I swore never to do it again, and I didn't.

Nonetheless, all the emotional upheaval from Marcia's death and my newly acquired wealth knocked me off beam once more. I just couldn't take the excitement.

I went into a decline so rapid it shocked even me. Alec was so kind. He encouraged me to let my fury flow. To scream, to cry out loud. He tried his hypnosis and massage treatments and didn't criticize even when I got falling down drunk.

Nothing made an impression until…

An unanticipated happening shocked me into pulling myself together, but fast.

Those sunny days and magical nights in Normandy had born fruit. I was expecting Charlie's baby - a seed, a part of him still alive and growing inside me. I needed so desperately to refocus.

Alec had taken to visiting on his days off. It was only a little over an hour's drive if the traffic was reasonable. It was an appalling waste of gas, but he did it anyway. He would stay overnight then set off back the following day.

I kept the knowledge of the baby to myself for a week or so without telling a soul. But I had to tell *someone* before I began to show, and I had every confidence Alec would be my friend in this as in so much else.

So, one day as we were walking in the woods, the woodland now glorious in its autumn hues, I stopped against a tree and looked down, shifting the yellow leaves around with my foot, and said:

"I have something to tell you, Alec."

I looked up but was having difficulty meeting his eye. He sighed.

"I know. You have a baby coming. I've suspected it for some time - it takes something drastic to turn a life around the way you have."

He hugged me to him and kissed me on the cheek, rubbing his face against my hair. I pushed away, the better to watch his expression.

"You're not angry? Not disappointed in me?"

"How could I be? War makes young people like us reckless when we may not live to see another day. You found that out to your cost. We fall in love quickly and completely."

I missed the implication. I had cause to remember it later.

"Come on. It's getting chilly and we've walked far enough. Let's go back."

He was strangely quiet and withdrawn as we strolled, so I put my hand in his.

Mr. Moffat had added to the total of my treasure a ten-thousand-dollar Ming vase he'd found beside the hearth. I shook my head. Marcia had been hopeless. She'd obviously had no idea of its value as the inside was coated with cigarette ash.

There were also a couple of somewhat depressing paintings by someone called Cezanne. They looked as if they could do with a good scrub – very dark.

While I was out checking the inventory of my fortune, Alec learned his mother was being repatriated the following week. He was cock-a-hoop.

When he went to pick her up in New York a few days later, I paced the garden, trying to work out what to do, when a voice with a thick German accent startled me.

"Mein frau... *Bitte verzeihen Sie die Störung*.... Don't be afraid. I won't harm you. *Herr* Maxwell once did me a great favor. Lotti is sick," he held out a dog for me to see. "I know he is a doctor. I wondered if he could help her."
I never in my life saw a dog with a more inappropriate name. It growled at me.

"He's a doctor, not a vet." I said nervously.

This bastard or his relatives might have been responsible for blowing Charlie to bits. I stepped backwards. When I was far enough away to feel safe, I snapped at him:

"What are you doing in this goddam country you son-of-a-bitch? Don't you know you're not wanted here?"

"*Ya*, I know," he said sadly. "But I will become American, ya? – I will work for papers. They put me in prison camp in Win-sor from beginning of *der Krieg* – the war, so I ran away. I am welder. I could have helped. I am no Nazi!"

He spat on the ground.

"My name is Dolph," he continued stoically.

Goddam. No wonder he was scared. His name was Adolph.

At that moment, I heard Alec's car on the drive. I ushered Dolph and Lotti – grrr – into the garden shed until I could assess the situation. Poor Janet. What had she come home to?

"Hello, dear Grace," she said, flinging both arms round me in exuberance, all twinset and pearls as usual.

I had decided to tell her about the baby. Afterall, within a few weeks she'd know anyway. I had no idea how she'd react. I'd give her a few days to settle in first.

Alec's family had now been restored to him, and for the first time, it dawned on me the Maxwells had gradually come to include me a one of their own. I was so desperately grateful to them.

I had the forethought to ask cook to set up a cream tea in the conservatory. It would look as if we'd picked up where we'd left off all that time ago, when Alec had first burst through the door with news worse than he ever could have imagined. For an hour at least, perhaps we could ignore the years between.

Janet, usually a woman of great strength, broke down and wept at the sight of the cake stands and delicate china, all set out for her favorite afternoon ritual.

When I insisted she pour, the requisite hankie was pulled from her sleeve, and she blew her nose loudly. Then she straightened her back and served us herself as she always had.

Each of us tried our best to keep the conversation light. Alec told of his hospital experiences but omitted to mention the battle fatigue and mental illness he had to deal with on a daily basis. Janet must have known an enormous amount about the bombing fatalities on English cities. And me?

Well… I had more than either of them to conceal – for the time being in any case.

I suddenly remembered Dolph. The poor man and his wretched dog had been sitting in a chilly garden shed for two hours. I tipped my head to Alec and looked meaningfully at the door.

"Excuse me, Janet," I said. I didn't give a reason and she didn't ask, just smiled into her teacup.

After I'd explained the situation, Alec ran round to the shed, unseen from the conservatory and opened the door. I followed at a jog. He was no vet, but he'd deduced the poor creature had a cancer, he thought in its stomach.

Dolph was devastated but asked if Alec could give Lotti an injection to take away her pain. Lotti gazed up at him with trust and adoration.

Alec retrieved his medical bag from the trunk of his car and gave the poor creature enough sodium amytal to fell a horse.

Presumably a smaller quantity had been meant for me. Although, after the conversation I would be obliged to have with his mother, a larger dose might be needed.

Dolph shook Alec's hand with tears in his eyes. We helped him bury Lotti and covered her grave with autumn leaves. Dolph stood silently for a moment or two, then loped off through the trees. We never saw him again.

I hoped when the War was over he'd fulfil his desire to become American as I so desperately wanted myself but suspected the bitterness left behind by the carnage would take a generation to dispel.

Chapter Nineteen

A Staunch Friend and a Revelation

I had purposely avoided telling Alec I intended discussing the baby with his mother. I knew he would be very nervous and try to talk me out of it. But it had to be done.

I found Janet on her knees planting spring bulbs in the border beneath the dining-room windows. She had on suede gloves to her elbows and black rain boots. She looked more as if she was about to hack her way through the Amazon jungle.

"Hello, dear," she smiled. "Pass me that trowel would you? My garden has been neglected for years and the soil is packed tight. I picked up some bulbs in England before I left – hyacinths and narcissi mostly. They should scent the room beautifully when the Spring comes."

I knelt beside her and picking up a hand-fork, started to turn the soil over so she could do her planting. She smiled her thanks.

"Janet. I have something to tell you. I hope you're not going to hate me for it."

I sat back on my heels and smacked the soil from my hands.

"Is it the baby, dear. Don't worry – I already know."

That Alec Maxwell was going to get a talking to for discussing me behind my back with his mother.

100

"Don't blame Alec. He hasn't said a word. I know the mannerisms of a pregnant woman - standing supporting your back, looking green in the mornings, crying a lot. Did you realize you did that? Most of us don't. I expect it might be difficult to tell one thing from another after what you've been through."

Despite what she said, I was usually pretty much in control of myself. The shock of losing Charlie had made me hard, but brittle. Tears of relief splashed down my face. This was one hell of a perceptive woman. I held her in greater respect.

There was silence for a few moments as we both concentrated on our individual tasks. Then she said, still working away:

"Have you had time to give much thought to what you intend to do about it?"

"Not really except I don't want the baby harmed in any way."

I paused, thinking through how I should go on.

"And was the father very charming? Frenchmen so often are. Very good looking too as a rule," said Janet without looking up. I sat back and regarded her in amazement. She gardened on. Was she psychic?

"I've been accused of that a time or too as well," she laughed.

But I hadn't said a word!

"I must teach you to use all your senses, but mostly smell and sight. Its easily done. More people should try it."

Janet stood and stretched.

"Let's go inside and have some tea. It's getting chilly out here. Would you like to discuss this further? If you'd rather not, I won't press you."

It was just so wonderful to unburden myself to such an understanding soul as Janet.

Dora brought tea to the sitting room and once she'd left closing the door behind her, Janet motioned for me to go on.

I told her all about Charlie. In passing, I mentioned his father. The only time she interrupted during the whole explanation was when she said:

"Ah, a Count. How thrilling. Son of the Duc de Riviere Beauvais? I used to play with Charles's aunt Charlotte as a child. She died of …. something or other, years ago. I forget what."

I looked at her with raised eyebrows. The world of European aristocracy is very small and often intermarried. Everyone English, even if they're from a smog-ridden city in the sticks is well aware of this.

She motioned for me to continue.

When I mentioned the canvas field hospitals and the mud and blood, I waited for some kind of sympathetic response, but she just stared stoically back. I'd a lesson well learned from her there and then. If you wish to be a comfort to someone, sympathizing was not always the right path. Sometimes it was better to just let them talk.

I didn't need to go into all the romantic stuff. She'd work that out for herself.

How to get through the next bit and stay sane? I'd done my utmost to forget, except when Alec dragged it out of me and made me face facts.

I took a deep breath and gritted my teeth.

"It's not an uncommon story in war," I went on. "It happens to lots of people but it's different when it happens to you. Charlie was working in the next ward to me. We were so busy we rarely saw each other except on a couple of days a month.

"Anyway, we were quite close to the front line near the Normandy beaches, and so busy I'd worked a forty-eight-hour shift straight. Then I just collapsed from exhaustion, and they carried me outside.

"Charlie saw me but had to return to duty when another convoy of wounded came in – he was on triage that day. He'd just got out of my sight when a shell destroyed both tents and everything and everyone in them. I was the only survivor."

"Then you have indeed been blessed to have a little piece of your love with you still."

How right she was.

"And what do you intend to do about this little miracle?" she asked over the rim of her cup.

"I'm alone, Janet. Charlie's child should have a good family to raise it, a happy childhood. I can't give it that."

"Adoption it is then? I suggest you have a good think about it before you make a final decision. Having a child taken from your arms is a physical pain. You must understand, your heart will break."

My head told me letting go was the right thing to do if I could.

"By the way..." said Janet as an afterthought. "You do know Alec's mad about you, don't you?"

I dismissed the remark as a joke.

Chapter Twenty
Devastation and Collapse

The total of my treasure including the Ming vase and paintings came to a little over eighty-nine million dollars. It was just a number - I had no idea how it would translate but it might be intriguing finding out.

My first ambition had been there since I'd sold bilberries I'd picked from Hardcastle Crags door to door for pennies in Halifax.

I'd never had anything of my own – something that belonged to me alone.

I'd start with a nice place to live. I hadn't really put down roots anywhere. Danbury, I suppose came closest, but it was 'a passing-through' sort of place - somewhere on the way to somewhere else. Perhaps I should move further west.

And after that what I'd like was another house. I was nothing if not thorough – or perhaps I was just becoming greedy.

The first should be a main residence. In the country but with ready access to a city. The second would be a holiday home, maybe the seaside or in the mountains. I'd heard the mountains were quite nice. I'd never been, so it was as broad as it was long.

The only place I'd been outside Connecticut was Chicago which was appalling. I wouldn't want to go there. Far too many dubious fat guys.

In idle conversation with Janet one day – we were making scones in the kitchen – I mentioned I'd been to Chicago with Marcia, and it scared me to death.

"There are some quite nice country areas around Chicago. It's not all gangsters and their molls," said Janet absently.

So, she hadn't recognized Marcia for what she was then. I hadn't worked out how to tell her about the diamonds, but now was as good a time as any, I supposed.

"Janet...." I stumbled for words. "Did you know anything else about her?"

"Only the usual gossip. Did away with herself, didn't she?"

She busied herself removing the cakes to a cooling tray and wiped the flour from her hands on her apron.

"She did. But she left me a bequest.... "

"That was kind of her, dear."

Now for the bombshell. I took a deep breath and straightened up as if I was about to march in a military parade.

"..... of nearly ninety million dollars."

I awaited her reaction. She was quiet for nearly twenty seconds while she bent to put another tray of scones in the oven.

"Did you hear me?," I said, uncomprehending. "Ninety million."

"I did, Grace. But I have been surrounded by wealth all my life and I can tell you without a doubt it's only worth what you do with it. Spend it dear, but wisely."

And that was that. She never referred to it again – not even to Alec.

We listened to the Japanese surrender at Tokyo Bay on the radio in Janet and Bill's sitting room. It wasn't until later I became aware of the devastation our bombs had wreaked, and later still when I truly understood the meaning of the sins of the fathers being visited on the children and grandchildren.

But like the rest of the country, I was jubilant our boys were coming home. Banners went up in the streets, fireworks made veterans duck with every bang, and there was a significant increase in the population the following April and May.

There was an enormous ticker tape parade in New York for the return of General Eisenhauer in June but unfortunately, I wasn't able to go. I was in hospital. My Katrina was born on June 11th, 1945.

She died in her crib the day of the tickertape reception for President Truman, October 27th. No-one could ever tell me why. All the doctors would say was that babies under one sometimes died without any apparent cause.

She didn't even die in my arms. I found her myself when I went to give her her early morning feed.

I chose to believe her Papa had come to take her home with him, for truly she was his child - the same indomitably cheerful nature, the same curling lashes, the same fine-boned frame. Perhaps heaven wasn't heaven for him without her. Perhaps I may join them some day. I hoped so.

So there I was, back to the beginning again, mourning another de Riviere Beauvais. This time with no hope for the future.

Of course, Alec was in a real panic about my mental health.

I would laugh and cry without apparent reason, I took to drinking cocktails at any time of day until my speech slurred. I had no concentration and would lose what I was saying mid-sentence, drifting off I couldn't say where. Between each bout I pasted on an apologetic smile.

Alec put me back on sedatives and his favorite regime of massage and hypnosis. It helped a bit but as he was obliged to increase the amytal dose, it was all a bit pointless, especially when I started hallucinating.

To make things worse, it was the most appalling weather in a decade. Great drifts of snow reached to the eves on the garden sheds and plopped from forest branches.

Janet had the parlor maid build a fire in my bedroom. It was warm and cozy and must have been most beautifully comforting, but I didn't notice. She would sit with me for hours on end, holding my hand, occasionally kissing my forehead.

The days passed and Christmas came. Bill, who had arrived home at the beginning of the month, carried a small forest pine into my room in an effort to please me. Alec tried to interest me in helping with the decorations, but I couldn't summon up the energy.

Then one day, when I'd clearly demonstrated – again – that sympathy wasn't necessarily the best policy, Janet lost her temper. I was making everyone's life a misery and it was after all, Christmas.

"Get out of that bed, you selfish brat," she yelled. "What bloody good do you think you're doing to yourself or anyone else for that matter."

I turned away, teary-eyed once more, and stared unseeingly out of the window.

"Didn't you hear me? Get....out.... of.... that...bed! NOW!"

She grabbed my arm and dragged me bodily from the bed. I lay on the floor, stunned.

"Now – get up!"

She dumped a box of tinsel in my hands and said:

"Get the fuck up and decorate that tree!"

That sentence alone shocked me back to reality.

I stared at her in disbelief. So did everyone else. The silence was deafening.

Then Bill burst out laughing and rocked with mirth until the tears ran down his face. Alec looked from his father to his mother to me, not quite knowing what to do next.

It was that which broke the ice for me. The look on his face was so funny, I began to laugh too. Or it may have been hysteria. In any case my mouth was turned up instead of down, which had to be a good thing.

Janet, alarmed at her temerity, was gazing at the openmouthed little group of servants who were hovering in the doorway.

"Go fetch some eggnog, Dora. And some glasses," grinned Bill.

"To hell with that!," said his wife. "Break out the Bollinger. Let's start Christmas early."

Then she turned and enveloped me in such a tight hug I had to push her away before I suffocated.

I wouldn't say my depression was cured after that – I shed many more tears over the next months – but I no longer felt my life was over.

Once the weather broke and the snow had gone, I went to cut kindling in the forest with Alec and we even had dinner in Danbury a couple of times. On one occasion I persuaded Janet and Bill to come too. They had been so kind. Janet secretly confided to me she too had lost a baby daughter although Alec didn't know.

It was Spring, the season of new life. For the whole world and me too.

Chapter Twenty-one

An Ambition Born for the 'Little Woman'

Then one day at the beginning of April, I awoke to a sky so ineffably blue it took my breath away.

I carried my breakfast coffee into the garden which was bathed in dew and sunlight.

The bulbs Janet had planted beneath the dining room windows had pushed through the earth and spread their unique perfume on the breeze. To me it smelled of England and a childhood of my imagination, the childhood I would have liked.

Trina would have been just starting to sit now. Maybe move around on her tummy. One day she would have a brother or sister for me to sing to on my knee. One day. But that was for the distant future. At the moment, Charlie's face haunted my every unoccupied moment.

Whereas I had always looked back, I felt this Spring morning belonged to my future. It was exhilarating.

Alec had been helping his father develop his clinic in Danbury. Bill didn't reapply for his hospital job in New York when he came back home after the war. He had seen the same appalling carnage as I had.

Often, when I started to look inward, he would pat me on the arm, give me a knowing wink and smile. I tried to do the same for him, but it wasn't often necessary. He was made of sterner stuff.

Alec was mostly working on rehabilitation programs for traumatized ex-GIs. Some would never get over it. He had had to come to terms with several suicides which he took as a sign of personal failure. These rocked him to the core. Then there would be several successes in a row, and he saw young men shaken by battle fatigue, return to family, take up jobs, marry wives.

But on this particular day, Alec came to me with a proposal. One that would do us both good.

There had been no new patients for a few days and his Dad had suggested he might like to take a little time to rest. He'd worked solidly since the end of the war, and it was true he was very tired.

"Why don't we do a road trip? You could check out America and maybe get to spend some money," he teased.

Sitting out in the garden on a sunny day the previous summer, when I felt the size of a house, I'd told him about my plans for new homes, plural. Saying it out loud made me feel so guilty. There was a time I couldn't even be certain of my next meal.

I thought it was a great idea. Just on the off-chance I might be able to make a hole in my inheritance, I decided to realize some of my assets.

Mr. Moffat had helped me open an account with the bank next to his office. On the say-so of Mr. Price who I'd authorized to sell one or two of the smaller pieces, the bank put forward a loan of fifty-thousand dollars to cover my expenses. Not long ago, my expenses had amounted to the price of a new shoe sole and a cord to tie back my hair.

So, while I skipped the light fandango round the lawn on that April morning, Alec loaded his station wagon to the roof with hats for the heat and hats for the cold, rubber boots and sandals and all the paraphernalia for a few weeks on the road.

Before we left, I took Alec's hand and walked down to the little chapel where Trina lay sleeping. Janet had had a little headstone made from pink marble. It was such a tiny little grave, situated under a sugar maple for summer shade and winter shelter. I knelt and kissed the little headstone and in my own mind said to her:

'Sleep well little one until your own special angel comes for you'.

It was just my fancy, a comforting thing to say to a little one.

I kissed the stone again, stood and went back to the land of the living.

I was so excited I couldn't keep still. Janet and Bill thought I was hilarious, but it was laughter tinged with love and who could object to that?

I couldn't even begin to remember the number of places we checked out. I rather liked the Susquehanna River in Pennsylvania, but Alec warned me not to start looking yet. There was an awful lot of America to see. It was just a tad bigger than England, which I took to be an understatement.

Understatement it most certainly was. I'd known it would be big, but I was awestruck at the sheer immensity of the country. Alec showed me a map. Once you actually got to a place with a name, it was okay. Everything was manageable. It was the distances between with absolutely nothing in them, not even any indication of habitation human or animal, which were incomprehensible. Hell, some places didn't even have plants.

In some towns, nothing much seemed to have changed. The old streets with wooden buildings which had once housed saloons and had horse-rails outside, were still clearly discernible. The ambience of the old West was very much alive. Gene Autrey would feel at home – so would Billy the Kid, although I saw no bars on windows.

Suffice to say, after a week's trawling round Pennsylvania and Ohio, we ended up – guess where? In Chicago.

I refused point blank to go into the city, convinced it was still full of fat middle-aged men with slicked back hair, which he thought so hysterically funny we nearly ran off the road. Once he had composed himself, he said:

"No, I don't think so. It's a different time now – they're telling the law they're legit businessmen so their profile is lower.

"But the areas I'm talking about are very rural and some of the houses overlook Lake Michigan. Let's go take a look."

"How do you know?" I asked, puzzled. He lived halfway across the Continent.

"I'd a friend from here who boarded at Canterbury, my school. I spent a couple of holidays with his family as a kid. Dad knew his father from med school."

I looked at him suspiciously. Why had he been so shifty about this? This was the first I'd heard of any friend.

He turned back the way we'd come for several miles and headed down a small country road with some pretty spectacular houses, all shiny and new. Except for one down a lane about a half mile further towards the lake. The turning could easily have been missed.

It wasn't for sale, but we looked anyway. It had something of the English country cottage about it although much grander. There was a pantile roof instead of thatch but a large garden with a stepped lawn.

The drive to the front door was lined with mature rhododendron bushes, brightly blossoming in the early summer sunshine. A path led round the side of the house and was covered by a trellis, laden with blush-colored China roses just coming into bloom. They reminded me of the ones outside the library window at Danbury House.

The house had an uninterrupted view across the lake and was surrounded by trees, which made it intensely private.

It was ideal. I could never have imagined such an ideal place if I'd thought for a thousand years. I wanted it from my soul. But it wasn't for sale. And even if it was, could I afford it? Damn, I could afford whatever I wanted. I just couldn't get my head around it.

Alec noted the acquisitive look in my eye and grinned.

"This is where my friend lives. Jack and I used to spend most of the summer splashing in the lake. It's freezing all year round."

"What do you mean? Do they still live here? Let's go then – you must be longing to see him."

Even I knew my enthusiasm was transparent. To hell with Jack – I wanted inside that house!

I spun round. A huge arc of cerulean blue stretched horizon to horizon without a single cloud. What I could glimpse of the lake between the profuse rhododendron blossoms looked calm and peaceful.

It was inevitable I would make comparisons. It made the bloodbath of Northern France and the smoke-fouled air and black brickwork of Halifax seem like dreams in another dimension. It was silent – well, except for the idiot humming mindlessly to my right. I dug him in the ribs.

"Be quiet. You're disturbing the peace!"

He picked up a large pebble from under the bushes and lobbed it with all his might overhead until it landed with a satisfying 'plop' in the lake.

"Told you it was close! Pretty good, eh?"

He was uncharacteristically excited. Even his own mother would never accuse him of frivolity. I thought of Charlie and me on that flower-sprinkled bank under a silver moon and knew instinctively romance was gone from my life forever.

The door had a knocker in the shape of a castle keep with a portcullis. Alec lifted it and let it go with an almighty bang.

"Strange door furniture, I've never seen anything like it before," I mused.

"Their name's McClean – it's their family crest. Don't let it worry you. We've got one too. It looks like a 'no entry' sign. They may have been impressive in the Middle Ages, but after the English knocked the stuffing out of us at Culloden, most of us ended up here."

"I suppose portcullises have a very limited use in Illinois."

The door opened with a groan.

"Alec? Alec, goddam man! What are you doing here? Why didn't you let me know? I'd have......," a man of Alec's age with wavy hair flopping over his brow and too-tight pants stood there. He was clearly Alec's opposite – ying and yang.

"Come in...come in..... Mom's not here but dad's out front. He'll be delighted to see you."

So far, he hadn't seem to notice me.

He ushered us through the foyer into a garden room overlooking the lake.

Andrew McClean was a tall, spare man in his sixties with a long face and an inscrutable expression. He wore a moss-colored tweed suit with elbow patches and had ink-stained fingers. He looked very academic.

Alec introduced me to Andrew who kissed my hand as if I was a real lady.

"And hello to you, my boy," he said shaking Alec's hand enthusiastically. "So glad to see you. Jack never mentioned you were coming. Jack, why didn't you say something?"

"Good reason for that, Dad. I'd no idea. Why had I no idea, Al?"

"Probably because I didn't tell you," said Alec dryly.

"Ah, that would explain it then," said Andrew McClean without a glimmer of humor.

"Jack, get Maggie to make coffee and... do you like muffins, Grace? I may call you Grace?"

"Oh, I wish you would. I keep looking round for someone else when someone calls me Miss Harper. And yes... I love muffins."

He smiled broadly. I got the impression he rather enjoyed them himself, but they were something of a treat.

Jack and Alec left to catch up on things and I went on chatting to Andrew.

"What's this about houses, Grace?" and at my enquiring look, "Oh Janet of course. The telephone was invented for people like her."

We smiled together in shared understanding.

"That's most interesting," he said. "I may be going through the same thing in a few months. Our secret, but I've been offered a job as a researcher at Harvard. I quite fancy going back to school but my wife might be less delighted."

He laughed but I got the impression he was worried about broaching the subject with his family.

"They'll probably be surprised, but don't you think they'll be pleased for you?"

"Oh, I don't know – probably. But I'm still nervous about it. We've been here for years, and you become set in your ways. But what about you?"

"A friend died recently and left me a sum of money. I've never owned my own home and thought it might be a good investment."

Jack and Alec came into the room at that point, in animated conversation.

"Idiot... you can't do that! What're you thinking?"

Jack punched Alec's arm.

"I know that," said Alec. "I thought Grace and I might fly to Denver, have a look at the mountains then on to the West Coast. We could pick up cars at the airports. Would you mind if I left mine here? I can collect it on the way back."

This was beginning to sound like a put-up job to me. I'd have liked a bit of discussion beforehand, instead of having him okay this with his friends, while I sat in the background like an afterthought on the purchase of my own house.

"I'm not so sure I want to do that, Alec. There are other places I'd rather see – like the Grand Canyon and Las Vegas. I've heard a lot about them. Mountains in Colorado sound dull."

I was irritated and Janet's coaching in how to stay in control had fallen flat on its face.

"I have to say I rather side with Grace on this one," said Andrew. "I'd be a bit annoyed at having my life sorted for me by someone else in front of people I don't know." This guy could become a friend. I smiled at him.

"Damn right, Andrew," I exclaimed. And there was no apology forthcoming for my language or familiarity.

Alec was going to have earache before we got to Denver – *if* we got to Denver. As I felt that moment, I might be flying back to New York – alone. I glowered at him a 'just you wait'.

The hall phone rang and Maggie answered it.

"It's Dr Maxwell," she called out. "For Mr. Alec."

Of course, I could only hear one half of the conversation Alec had with his Dad, but I rather gathered he was expected home.

"They've been overrun with ex-war casualties. They couldn't cope in New York so Dad's taking as many of the overspill as he can. The trouble is, many of them have psychiatric problems and that's my department. We'd better go Grace."

I was so disappointed I could have wept.

"Couldn't I go ahead alone? Then you could come out later when things have quieted down a bit?"

"Yes, I could run you to O'Hare," Jack remarked tactlessly. Alec ignored him.

"The times of Butch Cassidy and the Hole in the Wall Gang are not long past, Grace," said Alec. "Hell, Wyatt Earp only died in 1929. There are plenty of shady characters still robbing at gunpoint."

"So, I'll buy a gun," I said, getting peeved again at being treated as a helpless little woman.

They should appreciate that getting across the Atlantic dragging a reluctant sister, living with a gangster's moll, not to mention sliding around in mud and blood in Normandy and losing the love of my life to a German shell, does not make for a wilting violet. But this time I remembered Janet's advice, kept my mouth shut and listened until he ran out of steam.

"Finished? I'll tell you what I'm going to do. I'm going back with you. Then I'm going to get my naturalization papers and buy a car and a gun. Then I'm driving to California if it takes me the rest of my life, and I have to fight off Frank and Jessie James and the Younger Gang….," *thank you, Hollywood.*

I could see Alec was fuming but unlike me, embarrassed in front of his friends.

"Andrew, Jack," I said, "Delighted to meet you. I hope we see each other again in less fraught circumstances."

As I flounced out of the door, I heard Jack laugh:

"Oh, I like her Al. She'll do you the world of good. Drag you out of the nineteenth century by the scruff of your neck!"

"Quiet!" ordered his father.

Chapter Twenty-two
Desperate Desires Achieved - and 'Windham'

We drove back to Annandale in half the time it'd taken us to get to Windham. I fumed all the way back – conversation was minimal and stilted. By the time Janet was greeting us at the door, *Alec* was the wilting violet. Janet hugged me, hiding a laugh behind a pretense of blowing her nose.

"What did he do?" she whispered at his receding back.

"Treated me like 'the little woman'," I glowered.

Far from being the protective mother, she howled with laughter.

"His Dad did that *once*. Emphasis on 'once'."

"Hungry?"

"Starving."

We went into the house arm in arm.

Alec came down to eat then retired back to his room to 'unpack'. I was glad of that.

I cleared the table into the kitchen, then shut the door to give us some privacy.

"I'm actually not unhappy we had to come back. It's just how I was told, that's all."

As was her way, she remained silent.

"I'd intended getting out of your hair once we got back," I explained. "Months have turned into years. I don't know how I have the nerve to ask, but could I impose on you for another few weeks? I promise not to intrude more than absolutely necessary."

Janet waited for me to continue:

"Firstly, I need my naturalization papers. I've been here since '36. With the War and everything there never seems to have been time."

"That won't be a problem. You were part of the War effort," Janet explained. "You get a free pass. All you need is a declaration signed by your commanding officer. You'll find him if you apply to the military records office."

"He was killed along with Charlie and the rest of the medical staff. I was shipped out unconscious, so I've no idea who took over."

"Don't worry – Bill'll sort it. I'll get him to fetch a copy of the declaration for you as well. He has a stack of them at the surgery. Then it's just of matter of taking the Oath and you're in. I take it that's not all?"

"No. My argument with Alec made me realize I need to give serious thought to my independence."

I thought she was going to explode with laughter. I'd been making a dent in her soft furnishings for an age, so I added quickly, "Even if I don't do anything about it, I do need to have the choice of what I do next."

I paused; afraid she might be offended after all her kind hospitality. I was forthright by nature. Usually I didn't care, but Janet had been more to me than a friend – more like a mother. Thankfully she took it in her stride.

"Will you teach me to drive if I buy a car? I learn fast," I added pleadingly.

"Any idea what you want?"

"I was rather hoping you could help me with that."

"If you're wanting to discover America, I suggest a station wagon like Alec's - plenty of space to stow things. Chevrolet have just brought out a new one- it's all metal. The Woodies are becoming old hat now – they don't last…. I wouldn't recommend one of those…."

That turned out to be a fallacy as it happened.

She rattled on. I was fascinated by how much she knew, although for the most part I'd no clue what she was talking about. When she got onto engine sizes and oil filters, I drew the line.

"I take it that's a yes?," I said.

"Try and stop me! Shall we go now? There's a Chevy dealership in Danbury. We'll just get there before it closes."

I was too tired from the journey and asked we went the following morning.

"Then will you teach me to drive?" I asked again. She was so excited at the prospect I feared for the chair she was sitting on. It had quite spindly legs and she wasn't a small woman.

I wasn't surprised to find breakfast ready and waiting at eight o'clock the following morning. Janet had clearly eaten and was sitting with her feet up finishing her tea.

On the drive into Danbury, she asked me what I'd thought of the McCleans. I told her I thought Jack would be okay once he'd matured, Marion was out, and I could see Andrew could be a good friend.

"Pretty astute assessment. Pity you didn't see Marion. She's very pretty in a Hollywood sort of way – more

Ginger Rogers than Ann Miller. Jack needs a bat round the ear. Marion's too soft with him – only-child syndrome. Andrew's a dear. Bill absolutely hates him," she turned to look at me and grinned ear to ear.

"Old boyfriend."

I laughed out loud.

There were three car dealerships in Danbury – the Chevrolet we'd discussed, a Pontiac and a smaller Dodge. The first car I saw was a shiny pale green Chevy Fleetmaster. I knew it was the one but couldn't deny Janet the pleasure of traipsing round the other two showrooms, while she told me in a very loud voice what was wrong with every model. Really, either the woman had no shame or the confidence of an aristocratic background – a bit of both, perhaps.

When she started calling the salesmen 'young man' I'd to turn my head away. She glided round the Chevy dealership like a ship in full sail; poking this, pulling at that, wiping away imaginary smudges on the pristine paintwork, her face screwed up as if she'd eaten a lemon.

I sat on one of the plush chairs and watched in admiration. I could learn so much from her.

The upshot of her efforts was that she managed to get two hundred dollars off the price of a sixteen-hundred dollar car, and an undertaking that that particular car be delivered to her address first thing the following morning with a tank full of gas.

At that point it would be tested, and if satisfactory the price would be paid in full.

The salesman looked as if he'd been put through a wringer. I think he'd have *given* her the car had she asked for it, just to get her out of the showroom.

Once round the corner and out of his view, she leaned against a wall and giggled:

"I haven't had so much fun since Andrew McClean chased me up a tree."

By the end of August, I had a brand-new shiny car I could drive and was a fully signed up American citizen. Halfway through my ambitions. Houses to come.

Then Andrew McClean rang to tell Janet he'd persuaded Marion and Jack that Boston would be a good idea, so he was a brand-new Harvard research professor.

Alec, Bill and I were still sitting at one end of their huge dining table when Janet came back. She gave us the whole story, finishing up with Andrew placing the house with a realtor for thirty-two thousand dollars. Janet thought that was outrageous.

Andrew had been a bit overawed by the sheer enormity of moving from a house they'd lived in for thirty years, but Janet told him not to be so silly and to think of it as an excuse to spring clean. He ended up getting a removal company to do the work for him. Marion wasn't good at that kind of thing and Jack was, well, just Jack.

"Call him back and tell him I'll give him twenty-eight," I said promptly. That sounded abrupt but in truth I'd been running it round in my head since he'd mentioned moving to Boston to me.

All three snapped round to check I wasn't joking.

"What?," I said. "He wants to sell a house, I want to buy one. What's the problem?"

"Well put like that there isn't one, I suppose. It's a bit remote though, isn't it?," said Bill

"Not from Chicago and its airport. And I now have a brand-new automobile. Ideal I'd have said."

"Why don't you leave it until tomorrow, dear. There's no immediate rush," said Janet. "Oh Lord, I'll miss you," her eyes filled with tears.

"Don't think of it like that. Think of it as a free lakeside holiday. But you're right – I am tired. Tomorrow it is then."

All three looked flummoxed by the perceived suddenness of my decision. I retired to my room and did a little dance of delight. I was going to be a homeowner.

It wasn't all optimism, though. I made a long daisy chain and draped it over Trina's headstone, and scattered blooms over the grave. I hoped she understood how much her momma loved her because soon I would have to leave her all alone.

I buried my head in my hands and wept. I thought of Charlie and all that he had meant to me. I could never be comforted, the pain of their passing would never heal, so I would just have to learn to live with my grief.

The purchase of the car had taught me a thing or two.

I called Mr. McClean and arranged a proper viewing. I begged Janet to come with me which she agreed to with very little persuasion. Bill and Alec had work commitments, so they were unable to come with us, much to Janet's satisfaction.

So, on a morning which started cloudy and cool and improved to cloudy and warm, Janet and I set off in my brand-new motor singing 'Zip-a-dee-doo-dah' at the tops of our voices and scaring the hell out of the local birds.

We drew into Andrew McClean's drive travel-stained and bedraggled three days later, and asked for bath, bed and food in that order. So, it was actually four days from setting out before we were ready for action.

Janet was keen we should both keep our mouths shut and let them do the talking. It was a mistake to sound too enthusiastic she said, but like that was going to happen when I was practically jumping up and down with glee.

Marion who did indeed resemble Ginger Rodgers, fixed us a breakfast which would have fed a battalion.

All I'd seen when I visited with Alec, was the dark wood hall with its carpeted stairway and oil-paintings, and the garden room with a glorious view across the lake. Not much on which to base an opinion, but I felt in my bones this house was right for me.

It was an old house, so it needed a couple of damp areas fixing, but I would organize the repointing of the exterior brickwork myself.

It was amazing how quickly I'd got used to being a multi-millionairess. It was as if I'd been born to it. No one had the faintest idea why I suddenly became helpless with mirth. I think they thought I was hysterical. They were absolutely right. In my brain were two side-by-side pictures – poverty-stricken Halifax on a smog-ridden evening, and Windham with its flowers and lake views.

After she'd sniffed at every room in the house, Janet kissed the McClean family with special emphasis on Andrew, and Marion drove us to the airport. Janet winked at me behind Marion's back as we left, which I took to mean she approved of my purchase.

That isn't to say the rest of my move was easy, but I felt so uplifted by life itself, it was difficult to be fazed by anything.

A month later the McCleans no longer owned Windham House. The name on the deeds, in copperplate hand, was Miss Grace Ellen Harper.

I moved in within a few days of signing the contract, opened the conservatory windows wide, and let in the chill October air. It blew through the house, invigorating and refreshing it and sealing it as mine. It was autumn now but when Spring awoke the flowers, I would fill my new home with their color and scent.

By April I had the basics of the move finished. I'd need to acquire more furniture and get the bathroom and kitchen replaced.

Janet had returned for a week to help me out just before Christmas. She fired all the McClean servants, then engaged new people: a cook, a parlor maid, a gardener to start with - "we'll fill in the gaps afterwards."

She scared the living daylights out of them all, and showed me how it was done, so I could carry on the tradition once she'd left.

So, I now owned a Chevy Fleetmaster, a beautiful house with a beautiful name in a beautiful part of America, I was an American citizen and still not quite twenty-six. I was such a success!

Chapter Twenty-three

Sex, Bridge and a Chortle for Janet

But reality has a way of biting back.

Once Janet had gone home, the house was so silent it was eerie. I began to think I was hearing things. I'd tell myself it was wind off the lake in the rafters. A door would creak then click shut as I walked past. The scratching of birds in the eaves became ghostly fingernails.

Then a cloud would cross the moon and momentarily plunge the house into inky darkness.

One night I was so scared, I slept on a bench in the garden, wrapped in a bed quilt.

That's when Alec came looking for me. He'd been to visit colleagues of his dad's at the specialist stroke hospital in Chicago. I wasn't expecting him, but he wanted to take me out to eat before they flew back the following morning. He rang for a couple of hours with no reply because I was shivering in the garden.

Alec knew I knew no-one yet and had no friends locally, so he drove over to check on me.

Eventually, he found me on the lake shore. The first flush of the sun was just starting to spread along the horizon. I was as white as a sheet and trembling visibly, so he carried me to my bedroom, wrapped in the quilt and held me until the blood began to flow again.

I slept against his chest, and when I awoke, my fears had subsided, and I felt comforted and warm. I kissed his cheek in thanks. He hugged me and his eyes travelled down to my naked breast where the coverlet had slipped away in my sleep. I saw his eyes mist over with desire and I sat up and covered myself. He sprang from the bed, embarrassed.

"I'll go and fix us some breakfast and give you time to dress," he muttered as he went out of the door.

I'd learned the delights of physical love from Charlie, and it was part of my loss. The pain of his death ripped through my heart again, and my body responded with it. But I cared too much for the Maxwell family to take advantage of Alec, so I determined to take my pleasure elsewhere if need be.

Conversation over breakfast wasn't a problem - there wasn't any - and afterwards Alec left for Chicago to fly home. He kissed me chastely on the cheek before he went, but he couldn't look me in the eye.

As I watched him drive off, it suddenly occurred to me he was no longer the boy with the missing button and acne. He was a mature man of twenty-eight. Most women would have found him very desirable with his fine blonde hair immaculately cut, and his stunning bright blue eyes. For some reason best known to himself he seemed to want me.

I was five-foot-two with shoulder-length auburn hair, a skin so pale as to be near-transparent and a sprinkle of freckles across my nose which I hated. I had no class, no style and no dress sense. That needed fixing.

But first I had to stop being intimidated by this house. I decided the ghosts were only the feelings left by the McCleans, who had lived there for thirty years. It was time to make it *my* house.

I had the exterior brickwork repointed and the roof checked over, then I summoned up my courage and walked to the smart new house next door and asked them to recommend a firm of decorators.

The hall was to be stripped of its paneling and painted a very pale blue – almost white. The stair rails were removed and new spindles, painted cream with a banister of polished beech, fitted. All the carpets were stripped away. I had parquet flooring installed like Marcia's, throughout the downstairs, with the exception of the garden room which had a large Persian rug, and the kitchen which was tiled.

I was spending money hand over fist. Time to get onto Mr. Price again. I asked him to sell the spider's web jewelry suite. It fetched almost half a million dollars. I transferred the money for the house in full to the McCleans, paid the tradesmen when the work was completed, and I was satisfied with the result.

Of course, at this point I called my mentor. Janet, her face alight with anticipation, arrived to help me choose furniture and soft furnishings. She'd brough with her two friends from Maine and her own housemaid.

We were back and forth choosing a suite for the garden room in a buttery chintz which glowed in the sunlight, beds, dressers, sideboards, cupboards, tables, chairs, wardrobes and all the other necessary paraphernalia. We even travelled to Vermont to pick up an antique console Janet thought an absolute must for the sitting room.

So, the end result of all the work was a house painted in light airy colors, a neat garden planted with spring bulbs and resplendent with magnificent rhododendron blooms, which threw back reflections from the lake.

And thanks to Janet, staff who did as they were told.

There were no longer creaks or groans - not one ghost.

All gone.

I invited Janet, and Jessie and Frances her friends, to stay for a few days, but they'd taken a couple of months out of their busy schedules to help me, so needed to be at home taking care of their own affairs for a while.

So, rather than being alone in a creaky old house, I was now alone in a pristine, newly decorated one. But I was still alone. I needed to make friends.

I sat in my sparkling new kitchen with a cup of tea and thought about it. When it started to get dark, I moved to the garden room with a gin sling without the lemon or bitters.

When I'd slept on the problem, I came to the conclusion that if I wanted to make friends, I needed a hobby. I bought some golf clubs and knickerbockers. I looked ridiculous so I threw the clothes in the trash.

I quickly discovered golf was considered a man's game and I attracted not a little amusement at my ignorance.

"I take it you guys are too feeble to take on a woman at this pathetic sport," I snapped, turned on my heel and flounced out to sarcastic laughter.

Janet would have been ashamed of me. I'd lost my temper.

What else?

Bridge? Why not? I could join a beginner's club.

I stuck with it for a while, but it was composed of tedious old dears with no conversation, and when one of them said:

"Oh no my dear. it really would be foolish to bid five no trumps on that hand. It's an impossibility. Here, let me help you."

I felt my temperature rise, but this time I kept my cool, stared at her until she started to wilt, then next time she made a bad mistake, said:

"Last rubber didn't exactly go to plan, did it? Better luck next time, *dear*." And left.

They were shit. I'd set up my own Bridge club. I'd call it the Windham Association of Bridge Specialists, subtitled 'Knowledge of the Blackwood Convention a Requirement'. I advertised it in the local press.

That brought them in.

I held a soiree for prospective members and signed up sixteen girls all my own age, with another couple on call in an emergency. I decided on twenty bucks annual membership, just to keep it exclusive. They didn't mind coughing up since they were all sick of the old hags in the usual run of societies. On top of that, I had a waiting list of another fifteen.

I went out and bought half a dozen baize-covered stacking tables and some chairs.

All I had to do now was learn to play Bridge.

I bought a couple of books. It looked interesting but not exactly brain surgery. I dealt the cards out on the kitchen counter and played hands against myself until I thought I had it. It took me a couple of evenings.

I rang round and set up our initial game for the first of the month when the membership was to begin.

We drew lots for partners. Poor old Evelyn, soon to become a good friend, got me.

After we'd played a rubber or two and I was fixing a few drinks, she drew me to one side and said:

"You've never played before, have you? Don't worry – the rest of them didn't notice. It's just that you hesitated on plays which should have been obvious."

I bit my lip. Shit, found out on the first outing.

"Don't worry. I learned the rudiments from a book too. But I hadn't as good a poker-face as you. I got caught in the first game. Let me know if you want me to come round and give you some tips."

I'd found a treasure – a girl as devious as me.

I also discovered how Janet had learned her 'psychic powers' – playing Bridge. Watch, listen, smell. It gave you such an advantage. I needed to hone my senses.

When they'd all gone, and I'd put away the cards, and Lucy my parlor maid had cleared everything else, I picked up the box with the subs in it. It contained three hundred and twenty bucks. I knew it would in my head, but when I emptied it out on the dining table, I was surprised it looked so much.

Next year, if the club was still going, I'd buy a trophy and put something by as a cash prize. This was more fun than I'd expected.

Evelyn started coming round on a regular basis and our little Bridge lessons were extended to lunches at local bistros – I wouldn't go into Chicago – where we'd eat things like snails and lobster tails, and occasionally we got truly the worse for drink.

On one occasion, Evie slept on the sitting room couch while poor Lucy had to get me up the stairs and dump me on the bed.

I was having fun. I'd found a personal stylist, late of Hollywood – or so she said. She fixed me up with appointments for hair, nails and makeup and a tailor for my clothes.

Lingerie and perfume came from Paris, France. Oh my, I was gorgeous! Anyone who said money can't buy everything was making a mistake. It could do anything but fill the hole left by Charlie and Trina's passing.

Tired out from all the activity after the next evening of cards, I decided I'd go and visit Janet, if she'd nothing else on.

She'd arrange to pick me up from New York if I could get to the airport in Chicago, so I packed a bag, had my hair done and called a cab.

Alec had driven her to pick me up, and there was a bit of difficulty, as neither of them recognized the new me to start with. Both of them looked startled when the penny dropped.

It was Janet who walked round me and whistled, not Alec who stood stiff and expressionless behind her.

"Good grief, Alec. Its only Grace. You've known her forever," she said.

I looked at Alec. His expression clearly said he'd only just met this particular version of little Gracie.

I smiled at him and took his arm. When he looked down at me his face was rigid. He patted my hand somewhat formally. Janet huffed. She had no patience with him when he was being defensive. She took my other arm and led me to her car, all the while keeping up inconsequential girl-talk Alec couldn't possibly take part in.

Eventually, he let go and walked behind us. He'd yet to utter a single word – not even hello.

"If it's a nice day tomorrow," Janet said, "I thought we might take tea on the lawn. What do you think? There are one or two neighbors who're bearable. I'll ask them over. Did you have a good flight? The war might have been tragic, but it did wonders for the civilian airlines."

It was nice to know she was pleased to see me.

God knows what I should make of Alec's reaction. He seemed to have become as wooden as a male Greta Garbo. Perhaps he preferred the old unsophisticated me. Well, he'd have to get used to it.

Some of the neighbors Janet had invited brought other women with them. I could tell Janet wasn't pleased. A woman called Mavis sniffed loudly continually, and another, Joan, added gin to her tea. She became jollier as the afternoon went on.

Dora had set the table with a variety of French fancies and shortbreads on stands, and cucumber and cream cheese triangles with the crusts cut off, and the bread cut wafer thin.

Bingley carried out a large tea urn. I watched him, admiring his skill in carrying such a heavy item with his nose stuck so far in the air. He deposited it on a table placed for the purpose. He filled Janet's teapot, turned and marched back through the open door like a soldier on parade.

Janet poured the tea into china cups so delicate they were almost transparent and placed each on a saucer. Once her guests were seated, cup and saucer in one hand and plate in the other, she proceeded to offer round the sandwiches and cakes.

Of course, those not within reaching distance of the table were hungry and embarrassed. To anyone who knew her, the laughter behind Janet's eyes was unmistakable – to those who didn't she was inscrutable and thoughtless.

I couldn't stand it. I made a vague excuse about visiting the lavatory and made a dash for the door.

Straight into Alec's arms. He grabbed me and dragged me out of sight behind the drapes, kissing me over and over, his breath becoming increasingly labored. It would be wrong to say I pushed him away.

When he began to get a bit too free with his hands, I reminded him somewhat breathlessly, he would give his mother's friends the vapors if we were caught.

Unable to stop himself, he dragged me into a small sitting room, jammed a chair under the handle, and continued where he'd left off.

'Oh hell', I thought, '…. why not?' and encouraged him to the point of no return.

I was surprised how good he was. Definitely worth a repeat, but not at that precise moment. We did repairs to our clothing, pasted on smiles, and glided out into the garden.

I thought we'd done a pretty good job of tact, but Janet smirked and rubbed her nose. Damn, her radar must have been humming loudly.

Alec greeted each of his mother's acquaintances – in other circumstances he'd have shaken hands - and disappeared at the first opportunity. I was sitting there with a fake grin desperately attempting small talk, while Janet chortled away inwardly at my discomfort.

Joan hiccoughed and dropped Janet's precious Minton teacup.

Chapter Twenty-four

San Clemente

Things went up or downhill from there on, depending on your point of view.

I'd always thought a mother would be scandalize at the thought of her son's sex life, but Janet seemed to find the whole situation comical. I think secretly she would have liked us to be together.

For decency's sake I did my best to avoid Alec and when I left at the end of the week, I heaved a sigh of relief. I'd gone to Janet for a rest – now I was going home to Windham for another.

The Bridge evenings continued as did my friendship with Evie.

She had an on/off relationship with a guy called Alan Wilson, who was some kind of minor entertainments mogul, as she described him. Seemed more like a dancehall manager to me.

I was quick to ascertain he didn't run one of the houses Marcia might have known, but I gathered he organized dance nights for young kids - the noisy kind with a big band and ex-soldiers intent on making up for lost time.

I accompanied her to a couple of evenings there, until she set up a foursome with one of Alan's creepy pals. He had greasy skin and body odor. Evie was disappointed - she would have liked us to get along – but no way was that going to work, and she could appreciate why. It was just easier if I stopped going with her, so we just did Bridge and eating after that.

One night when I was least expecting it and was clearing up after Bridge, who should arrive but Alec. He was carrying a bunch of flowers so enormous I had to stand on my tiptoes to see who it was when I opened the door.

He gave them to me with a kiss, took them back then walked into the kitchen and placed them carefully into the sink which he half filled with water.

Janet's teaching on sensory perception had started to kick in now, and I eyed him speculatively. He glanced away when he spoke to me and smelled nervous. We'd only had a quick if passionate moment of mutual attraction at Annandale. I'd quite fancied a repeat at the time but hadn't dwelled on it much since. Was that what he was here for?

I made coffee for him but he seemed particularly distracted, so conversation was stilted. How had we become strangers to each other? We'd always been such good friends, and I had so many reasons to be thankful to him.

The girls were still clearing up from my little soiree, so it was difficult to speak privately. I took pity on him and suggested a walk down to the little private beach on the lake shore.

We'd hardly set foot on the sand when he pulled me into a demanding kiss. It struck me I was becoming for him what Charlie had been to me.

We made love, less violently now we had privacy. I needed this as much as he did.

After that, Alec was a regular weekend visitor. Sometimes he came, spent two hours and took the next plane back. The end result of our lack of self-control was obvious.

Alec and I married the following March. Janet wasn't happy about it, mostly I think because she understood he was second choice. She knew in my heart I had never given Charlie up, and probably never would. She wanted more than that for Alec and so did I. I was most heartily sorry for the whole mess.

Our wedding at Annandale was small, but Janet still managed to make her garden a magical place. She hung the trees with candles in jars like so many fireflies, set out tables for the few guests we had and filled them with.... cream tea and a six-foot tall five-layered cake decorated with orchids, and blush-colored rosebuds which matched my bouquet.

Alec was intensely shy with me for quite a long time. I think he blamed himself for our state of affairs, but I didn't really know why - it took two, after all. I guessed he was old fashioned in his outlook and believed a man should be answerable for all aspects of his behavior.

He seemed constantly to be apologizing to me for something... anything. In the end I lost my temper and told him we had a situation we were both responsible for creating, and we'd better learn to deal with it. His mother liked that, but Alec seemed offended.

Of course, the passion in our love life had fizzled. Unwarranted responsibility has a way of doing that. I didn't know if it would recover over time, but probably not. I couldn't bring myself to care one way or the other. It had just been stupid lust brought on by loneliness on my part. On his side, I do truly believe he loved me, but there was no purity to it, no control. If love couldn't be, respect was the next best option and that should be possible from us both.

I was starting to show, so we went about as far away from Annandale as we could get and took our honeymoon in California. Just a matter of sticking a pin in a map, we ended up in San Clemente, a small Spanish-style town between the cities of Los Angeles and San Diego.

It had been built when the owner of the outrageous oil derricks that packed nearby beaches up the coast before the war, perhaps in a moment of guilt, decided to reinvest some of the huge amount of money he'd made, into creating something beautiful for his workers. Or perhaps he just couldn't find anything else to spend it on.

I fell in love with San Clemente the moment our cab pulled up outside the hotel, which was beautiful, old-fashioned and painted white in the Spanish style.

On the first day, we spent time examining the shopping area and checking out the highly ornamented churches.

When we tired of the town, Alec and I walked the bluffs on the coast to the north. They gave a magnificent panorama of the azure ocean, hazy in the sunshine, and the town below with its golden sandy beaches and magnificent pier. There was no doubt in my mind – this bluff and I shared a future.

I'd overdone it striding about in the heat of the day, so of the two left, the first was spent resting in our room. But we couldn't leave San Clemente without walking the pier, so late on the following afternoon, we viewed the entire panorama of this stunning part of California's coastline from its rail. I made a mental note of the position of my future villa, picturing it in my mind to the last detail.

Janet and Bill had opened up the house for us when we got back to Windham. I asked her to excuse me and went to bed. Tomorrow would be soon enough to start World War Three.

"Why not, Janet? Plane travel is improving all the time. Its only very new and a bit experimental, but they've introduced cabins where you aren't frozen to death and thrown about like ping pong balls. Think of it - two thousand miles of sitting with your feet up." Never one to miss a trick, she said:

"I look forward to watching you entertain a baby from Chicago to Los Angeles."

"No problem. I'll fill its bottle with gin."

"Don't be flippant – there are two other lives to consider," she said seriously.

"Where's your spirit of adventure, Janet Maxwell? You must be getting old."

Telling a woman in her sixties she's getting old is about as dangerous as telling a teenager they're immature. She puffed out her chest, screwed up her eyes and instantly became incoherent.

"Why you…. You….," words failed her.

"Windham has been such hard work," I carried on serenely, "I really would understand if you didn't feel up to it. It's not a problem – I'll call Evie."

Her radar told her I was laughing at her which she found infuriating. Of course, that was the whole intention. She knew that too.

Our little boy was born in September at Windham. We named him Oliver Harper Maxwell. He was quite beautiful - fine white-blonde hair with Janet's bright blue eyes. He was a placid child, not given to extremes of emotion. Even as a baby he seemed to spend a lot of time alone, locked in his own thoughts.

Windham flourished with the new life within. Or perhaps it gave Alec and I a common interest, something to talk about. Things between us did gradually improve and we at least became friends again – very good ones for a while.

We didn't have a completely platonic marriage but it wasn't satisfactory. I don't think either of us would have minded the occasional fling provided it didn't interfere with our life at Windham, but I certainly didn't go in that direction, and I don't think Alec did either.

Alec's expertise with mental illness had now extended beyond war casualties, and he had gained quite a reputation as a pioneer in an important new area of medicine. Because of his extensive experience, he was offered a research fellowship at the university in Chicago.

Academia was not a comfortable concept for him, so within a couple of years he had left to set up his own private practice. He advertised in a medical journal for a junior doctor willing to be trained in his working methods and was overwhelmed by the response.

His eventual choice was a young man of twenty-three called Freddie Freeman. He'd have scared me to death. He had degrees from Harvard and Oxford and his intellect was a sharp as a razor. He was clearly bent on sucking Alec dry of information. Alec thought he was wonderful, and I must say, they worked together very well.

Originally, Alec had planned to work from home, but the house proved impractical for a surgery, waiting room and pharmacy. He resorted to running his practice from a rented unit within the university complex, until he could find a suitable unit to buy.

Despite his professional commitments, he was a very hands-on father. Alec wasn't above rolling around on the floor with Oliver or building towers of wooden bricks for them both to knock down with a clatter. Oliver would shriek with laughter. It made my headache.

He loved to crawl round the garden and when he was bigger, tottered round the lawns under the watchful eye of the gardener who should have been working, but took every opportunity to play dens with him beneath the rhododendrons.

Older still, and Oliver would build a little play parlor hidden beneath the bushes, with cushions filched from the sitting-room, water in soda bottles and old cups. He would disappear into his secret world for hours at a time, until dusk or hunger brought him to the house.

We only had one mishap, when he fell into a patch of nettles when he was hiding from his nanny behind the potting shed. His scream could have been heard in Chicago.

And while Alec's star was rising, mine had sunk without trace. My poverty-stricken childhood had each family member toiling to keep us clothed and fed, then I was a servant and after that came the war. There had been no time to be lonely.

Lately, I had been preoccupied with my pregnancy and taking care of a tiny baby. Now he was older, and we had employed a nursery maid, I wasn't needed so much.

Chapter Twenty-five

'Windham' – Alec, a Pain in the Ass

I found Oliver's self-possession irksome. Although it's a terrible thing to admit, I loved my son but had no liking for him. I often wondered how I would have felt about Trina but loving her could only have been part of my devotion to her father. Perhaps that was the problem I had with Oliver. With Alec there was plenty of respect and appreciation but no warmth.

So, there was no other way of construing future happenings - I had a hand in the calamity to come.

Once Oliver started school, I decided it was time to get my California dreams back on track.

Of course, after the jibes I'd made about Janet's age, she was backwards and forwards to Windham on a regular basis.

For almost a year she practically lived with us which was just fine by me, but because she came down firmly on my side in any disagreement, Alec called her 'an interfering old bat', and each time wanted to see the back of her as soon as possible. Of course, that was water off a duck's back with Janet. She went temporarily deaf quite often.

I contacted the agent for the piece of land I proposed buying on the bluff overlooking that intensely blue ocean, with its mewling gulls and ribbons of golden sand.

The land was available to buy but was bound by so many rules I was at first outfaced. Once I'd come to terms with the broader picture, it became easier.

San Clemente took its name from the tiny island just offshore from the town. Things have relaxed since, but when I was looking to buy, there were strict regulations about the appearance and design of the Spanish style houses.

I considered buying a ready-build – even saw one I quite liked, but recognized I was swayed by the cerise and violet bougainvillea hanging in festoons from its wrought-iron balconies.

I employed a surveyor who told me the land was unstable and wouldn't take the weight of a villa where I wanted it. Although it would impede the perfect view, I agreed to it being moved back fifty yards which meant its rear was right against a sheer rock wall.

I took a bottle of coke, a peanut butter sandwich and a shooting stick and spent a couple of hours getting a feel for the place. The back of the house against the rock would be very cool, I thought. It would be perfect for Marcia's books - free of moisture and with a constant temperature.

I could even incorporate the stone face as one of the room walls. Now that would be interesting. Yes, and a couple of easy-chairs and a central table. I'd have to think with the lighting though, as there could only possibly be one window. The lighting would be important - perhaps reading lamps would work and a spiral stair to a roof terrace.

I wasn't much concerned with the house itself, other than it had all the usual offices and four ensuite bedrooms.

By the terms of the purchase, the house must have the exterior in the Spanish style, so I had it painted white, with colored tiles on any steps, and lots of arches. The architect could fix that. It would need a small suite for servants and a garden house to the rear for guests – if I had any.

What did concern me was a terrace out front. It should be as big as possible to contain all the accoutrements of outdoor living. The architect said the only way we could do that safely was to fit it with concrete palings to support the weight at the front, but that would leave an open space beneath.

I was fine with that. I could put Oliver there when I got sick of his yelling. With his nursemaid of course. Then I could sit on my terrace with an ice-cold drink and gaze across the Pacific in peace and quiet.

That left the gardens.

The road up to the house was steep, so I had a zig-zag drive made to the front door. I would plant it with rhododendrons like the ones at Windham, and lower growing hydrangeas for their brilliant color.

I suddenly realized I was singing away at the top of my voice. I was loving this.

At last, time intervened and I'd to go. I'd let the architect get on with his job and gave him permission to employ the necessary contractors, artisans and so forth on condition he ran the accounts by me first. Despite my move to Illinois, Mr. Johnson in Danbury was still my attorney. He could take care of all the legal stuff.

Yes, this was all coming together nicely. I'd be able to present it to my mother-in-law as a fait accompli. She would have no hand in its design – it would be all my own work. I had a passing thought she might not like being left out, but I dismissed it immediately.

So back to completing Windham and immersing myself in the *really* enjoyable bit – knickknacks.

Janet had bought me the most beautiful Minton tea-set as a wedding gift – much like the one her neighbor's friend Joan had smashed on the lawn at Annandale. I rather gathered cream-teas were expected to be a regular occurrence in Illinois too, especially as she'd bought a pair of matching cake stands as a house-warming gift.

Marcia had had a predilection for Chinese porcelain which I shared. The blue and cream color scheme would look spectacular in the hall and would be the first thing seen on entering the house. I had a cabinet maker construct display shelves and started my collection. Not all at once. I'd shop around.

In all, I spent a hundred thousand dollars on antique china, ornaments, water-colors and a few pieces of furniture I didn't need but couldn't resist.

That included a Louis Quinze tapestry-upholstered sofa with goldleaf cherubs. It was so delicate I was terrified someone would sit on it, so it ended up in my bedroom. Still, it was nice to think it may once have been graced by Madame Pompadour's posterior. I excused my extravagance by telling myself it was a good investment, although at seven thousand dollars, I doubted it. That was the Yorkshire woman in me speaking. An old sofa was an old sofa.

I spent some time in New York poking around in junk shops, occasionally turning up something worth having. Janet would join me for lunch at the Carlisle on Madison Avenue, where I'd stay overnight before flying back home.

Before long I realized I'd filled every surface in every room with bits and pieces, had installed all the lamps, shades and chandeliers, laid all the rugs and displayed all the china.

Alec wasn't impressed. He said he was afraid to turn round in case he broke something. But he was just being cantankerous – his mother's house was stuffed with antiques.

Oliver was more of a problem. As far as he was concerned, I'd turned his home into a museum. On one occasion, I saw him quite deliberately smash a Wedgewood vase against a window in temper. When I strode into the room in fury, he looked me in the eye and said: "Oops."

I walked round the garden for half an hour trying to quash the desire to beat him black and blue.

To my absolute fury, his daddy took him out for a knickerbocker glory. He could play us like a piano. Which reminded me, I didn't have one of those, so I bought one. A white baby grand imported from Italy.

Chapter Twenty-six

San Clemente Complete with Tina

It didn't take long for me to need a break, so I flew out to California to visit the architect and check on the progress of the house in San Clemente.

Much to my surprise its construction had moved forward quickly. I was delighted with the terrace which took up almost a quarter of the total floor area of the whole building.

We discussed my thoughts for the library and I explained what I wanted. He liked the idea of incorporating the cliff face into the rear wall but said it would be better to veneer it with marble, as the rock on its own would crumble over time.

Another couple of months of to-ing and fro-ing and it was finished.

I put in a team of cleaners, then had the inside painted white, with red tiles and lots of chrome in the kitchen. I fitted the house bathroom with a tub Cleopatra would have chosen for bathing in milk.

The terrace had a whole wall of sliding glass windows, so the inside and outside could be joined together.

Then I went to Los Angeles and looked out furniture for the terrace.

I found an Italian tiled table with six matching chairs in a back-street boutique. It was black wrought iron with bright blue tiles with splashes of yellow. It was absolutely completely out of place with the rest of the rather sedate terrace furniture I'd found, but perfect for canapes on summer evenings.

Black-pudding to canapes – who ever could have imagined it? I wondered what my Dad would have thought of Alec and Janet and the house at Windham, never mind this bit of expensive frippery in Southern California.

Perhaps I should send money to lighten their load. I'd have a word with Mr Johnson to post some pound notes in an envelope every month – my Dad had never crossed the threshold of a bank in his life.

The town had its human ants scurrying below, much as those I'd watched with Charlie on the castle walls in Caen.

All my joy was wiped away in a flash, replaced by a despair so deep I was numb.

But I'd go crazy if I allowed myself to go down that road, so I squared my shoulders, tossed back my head in defiance and flew back to Chicago.

As the only person who could possibly understand my yearning for a man dead years ago was my husband, there was nothing I could do to cope but shove my feelings deeper and deeper.

I knew I was becoming hard and unapproachable – sarcastic, even. There didn't seem to be a thing I could do about it. The only person I could cry to was Trina, and every time I visited Janet, I spent an hour on my knees at her grave. When I knew no-one could see, the tears coursed uncontrolled down my cheeks. They'd gone and left me behind.

I began to notice the lines already etched in my face had deepened, and my hair was becoming prematurely silver. To compensate, I spent more time at the beauty parlor and with my dressmaker.

At Windham I learned to know my son again.

He never was an academic child, much to the chagrin of his teachers. He was clever but math, literature and Spanish bored the pants off him – he'd rather be swimming in the lake or pitching a baseball, either alone or with his father.

Alec spoilt him dreadfully which meant hope of a comfortable marriage was dead in the water. Any attempt by me to instill discipline was destroyed by Alec's willful behavior. He quite deliberately used Oliver as a stick to beat me with. I'd thought we'd both come to terms with our situation, but it seemed we'd *both* been guilty of buried feelings.

After a while, when I started tearing my hair out, I went back to San Clemente. Alec, unable in the school vacations to control Oliver any longer, took him to stay with his parents at Annandale.

The first week at San Clemente was spent interviewing staff. I needed people I could trust as I would be away for long periods in Windham. There seemed to be a rotating pool of servants in the town who moved from one employer to another. Those wouldn't do at all.

I looked further afield and included some of the rural areas in my search. San Clemente was situated in Orange County, which was indeed the county of oranges, with row upon row of fruit trees with here and there a vineyard. The buildings were mostly single story and painted white. The overall ambience was one of peaceful order.

But although the fields were orderly and well-taken care of, the workers seemed gaunt, clad in worn overalls; the men with old battered trilbies and the few women ill-kempt, and with their skinny children, prizing stones from between the tree roots.

I pulled into the fount of all knowledge in small town America, the local drug store, and bought a couple of packs of cigarettes. Lighting up, I casually asked the counter clerk if there was an employment agent in town.

"No Ma'am," he replied, "But you could try asking for Mitch Torrance at the Livery Stables." *Livery Stables?*

The Livery Stables turned out to be a diner on a small street of clapperboard houses, swept clean and planted here and there with bright geraniums.

I ordered a coffee and a chicken sandwich, ground out my cigarette in a tin ashtray and looked about me. There were one or two other customers, mostly teens with milkshakes and big grins.

The waitress was smart, clean and rolled gum skillfully round her tongue. I was immediately reminded of Lon. One of the kids called out:

"Hey Mitch! Got dimes for the record machine?"

So this young girl with great legs and a checkered skirt was Mitch Torrance? I'd been expecting a middle-aged cowpoke.

"Y'all jest quiet down while I serve this lady," she said.

She turned her back on them, put my food on the table and smiled at me.

"I just moved to San Clemente, and I need to find reliable live-in staff," I said. "The ones already in town won't do – at least, I didn't like them. The clerk at the drugstore recommended you as the person who might know of anyone suitable locally."

She asked my permission then slid onto the seat opposite, resting her chin on her cupped hands.

"That's on account of everyone passing through here sooner or later. It's got to be a regular gossip hotspot."

"Ain't that the truth," laughed a voice from behind her.

"There's one or two," she mused. "Best bet's prob'ly Tina Lopez. She lost her husband last year and her only kid left town. Hasn't been seen since. She's smart and honest s'far as I know. Leave your number and I'll have her call you."

"How about you?" I asked.

There was a loud guffaw from the kids. She gestured for silence.

"Sure's a great idea, but I'm stuck with this place so not a possibility."

She owned it? She couldn't have been more than twenty.

Two days and one phone call later, I was interviewing a small Mexican lady called Tina Lopez. She was shorter than me which immediately gave me a superiority complex – not many people were. She looked absolutely scared stiff.

"Oh, my Lord, Tina – despite appearances I'm not Dracula's mother!" – *I might be rethinking that –*

158

"Would you like something to drink? Brandy, Bourbon...? Just calm down. If I can't understand what you say, how can I learn what you can do?"

"Si, Senora... as you wish Madame. Mada......."

The more nervous she got the thicker became her accent and the more Spanish she interjected until we were both as confused as each other.

Terror aside, she looked clean and capable, and I was sure one of us would come to terms with the other's language eventually. She worked for me for years, but she never got over her fright and would drop things in a panic if I came within ten yards of her.

Once she'd agreed to a live-in status, I bit the bullet and had a local attorney draw up a contract of employment, and using my experience of working for Marcia, bought her work clothes.

Then I rang Janet with my 'fait accompli'.

Chapter Twenty-seven

A Spoilt Brat, a Daughter and her Angel

Janet was so relieved to leave Oliver with Bill and Alec, she was in Los Angeles two days later. Thank God for pressurized cabins!

She did her usual nose-in-the-air sniffing as she walked around, which I now knew to ignore. She stopped however, once Tina put a jug of iced mint tea on the terrace table and, glass in hand, she stood at the rail looking over the sweeping ocean and town far below, lights beginning to twinkle in the twilight. Then she turned and looked at me, wide-eyed.

"But it's absolute perfection, my darling. Whyever didn't you tell me?"

"Janet, it's years since I first told you!"

"Our bolt-hole is out of this world. I'm exhausted. Where's my room?"

She sank the rest of her drink in one.

Once I'd taken the 'our' in, I showed her to the semi-derelict room Tina and I had scrubbed out for her and apologized.

"Does it have a clean bed? That'll do. Other problems are for the morning. Goodnight."

Janet now took over – this was her forte after all.

The following week I had a cook, gardener with his son as assistant and paid from his father's wage until he proved himself – I rescinded that immediately - and another housemaid on my payroll; all sorted out with contracts and uniforms and instructed as to their responsibilities.

Tina and Tomasina who was immediately dubbed Tommy, were to move into the servant's suite and put in charge of housekeeping. I paid a security guard to work overnight in the grounds.

The decorators were given a rocket up the derriere and finished their work in double time, while Janet and I ate fish suppers on the pier and went shopping in Los Angeles.

I put the rest of the staff on permanent paid retainer. Tina was to contact them with details of my return. Janet recommended I put a clause in their contracts that anyone not turning up when needed would find themselves instantly dismissed without a reference.

Once she'd sorted me out, Janet went home. She loved to feel useful and hated to sit still for too long. I spun out my stay as long as I reasonably could, then packed up and went home to Windham.

While I was away, the springtime garden had exploded into a riot of color and perfume. Larkspur in abundance had erupted beside the gate, blue, mauve, white and pink. The roses on the trellis were just coming into bloom and my rhododendrons, heavy headed, lined the lakeside path. Night-scented jasmine spanned both sides of the main door and the lawns were trimmed and smooth.

I could hear Bill and Alec with Oliver on the shore. Alec and his Dad sat on loungers and Oliver was in the lake, all snorkeled and flippered up. It must have been like the north pole in there, but it didn't seem to bother him. When he saw me, he splashed his way out and ran up the beach, grinning.

"Look Mom, look what I caught. Isn't it something?"

Between his cupped hands was a small minnow, flopping its panic over and over against his palm.

"Go put it back in the water and let it swim away" I said firmly. "You're hurting it."

His bottom lip stuck out and his eyes screwed up.

"Won't. Its mine. I'll say what happens to it."

"It's dying, Oliver," said Bill.

"So what?" yelled Oliver rudely. "There's plenty more of them."

He threw the poor little thing down on the sand, where it continued to flop feebly, and marched back to the house in a temper.

Alec strode over, picked up the poor minnow and tossed it back into the lake.

"I suppose he's right in a way," said Alec. "There are shoals of them – look."

Yards from the shore was a school of tiny fish, jumping and flashing silver in the sunlight.

"That's not the point," I ground out. "He needs to learn respect for all living creatures. Even the ones with a few spares. I'm going to bed. See you…… whenever."

As I turned, I just caught the look of alarm Bill flashed Alec's way.

Janet's delight at having three houses to flit between was apparent, but eventually she had to make a decision as to which was her home. Of course, she settled on Annandale as the name on the deeds was William Simpson Maxwell and she did after all, at least like her husband.

Bill was able at last to leave the Maxwell family junior at Windham for the summer.

It was Oliver's tenth birthday at the end of September. I offered to take him to San Clemente to have a beach party before he went back to school, but as usual he chose to do something else. All he could be persuaded to do was visit Grandpa Maxwell and Uncle Duncan – no mention of his grandmother. Janet was no easy touch, and Bill and Duncan tended to treat him more as one of the boys than Alec did.

Alec was busy working, so I drove Oliver to Annandale myself. All the way, he didn't speak unless spoken to, and irritated me by repeatedly turning up the car radio to deafening. But I stuck to Janet's code and didn't react, so eventually he got bored with that, and took to humming tunelessly instead.

I was delighted to see Janet and Bill again. Janet took my arm and fixed me a stiff whiskey. I knocked it back and she refilled the glass. I began to unwind.

"That bad, was it? What possessed you not to fly?"

"Worse than you could possibly imagine… a nightmare. I thought a drive might do us good – you know, sort of a mother son thing."

"Most unlike you." She raised an eyebrow.

"I've been at San Clemente so much, I guess I was feeling guilty. God alone knows why!"

At that moment, Oliver ran into the room and flung his arms round Janet's neck

"Granny, Granny – its ages since I saw you."

"I've missed you too," replied Janet without expression. Fortunately, he wasn't old enough to appreciate the irony.

"Now, off to bed. You've both had a long journey. Tomorrow is soon enough for adventures. Off you go," and she waved him off with her fingers.

He looked mutinous for a moment then shrugged and did as he was told. Too tired to argue, I guessed.

"Will you go to see Trina now, or after you've rested?" asked Janet, quietly.

"Both, I think."

"You know you have to let that little girl go, Grace. She needs to sleep, and you won't let her be."

I'd never thought of it that way before.

"I will," I said. "In a little while." Letting her go would mean letting Charlie go as well, and I didn't know if I could.

Later, I knelt alone on the grass by Trina's gravestone, cleared away dead leaves and old flowers, then planted my pocketful of crocus bulbs. It broke my heart that her Papa's name couldn't be written there. The text read:

Katrina 'Trina' Maxwell

Beloved daughter of

Alexander and Grace Maxwell
and dear sister of Oliver

Taken from us October 27th 1945

Wait for the Angel's glow

Oliver, of course, knew nothing about her and would never dream of setting foot here anyway. He had a horror of graveyards. Too many evenings with Alec and Bela Lugosi, I suspected.

I didn't know why I had this picture of a bright Angel in my head, but occasionally he would appear in my dreams and would confuse me. I could almost touch him. He had the softest of blue eyes - never demanding, never questioning. I called him the angel because his whole being was suffused with a gentle glow. But he filled me with pain too, because I knew one day he would come, and Trina would leave with him.

I was not a fanciful person – never had been, never would be – but for some reason the angel was as real to me as the people at Annandale.

I bent my head and great silent teardrops welled from deep inside and splashed on the earth. I couldn't give these tears to Oliver. He was as distant and cold as snow on a mountain. I could never break through his shell.

"Your grieving has gone on for long enough," said Janet, bluntly, on my return. "It's time to look to the living."

She realized the import of that remark – that I had no one to turn to - and pulled me to her.

"You'll always have me, my daughter. Family isn't always blood."

That was exactly…. precisely what I needed to hear. She never failed me, and I loved her like the mother I'd never known – more, probably.

"Will you come with me to say a final goodbye?"

I needed to be alone when we got back to Annandale. I went to my room, lay on the bed and stared at the wall. I was all cried out.

Eventually I fell into a troubled sleep, during which her angel held my little one in his arms and whispered in his loving way, promising he would bring us together again.

I would know when he came for me he said, 'by the music of the stars, and seeing his own beloved child's first understanding.' Whatever that might mean.

He seemed peculiarly anachronistic, as if he gazed into the future, which was odd, since he held my past in his arms.

After that, I slept soundly and didn't wake until the following dawn.

The house was silent, so I dressed and walked through the woods to where the trees thinned. I sat on the soft earth and watched the September sun rise majestically above the horizon.

The world awoke. Birds sang, flowers unfurled their satin petals, and I saw a doe tentatively stare at me through the undergrowth – a rare sight indeed.

I was amazed to find rather than overcome with sadness, I actually felt comforted.

Chapter Twenty-eight
Oliver and 'Canterbury'

That evening Alec flew in for Oliver's birthday. He was just in time to kiss him before Janet wrangled him into bed and read to him from Edgar Rice Burroughs. I was beginning to develop a real liking for 'John Carter of Mars' – he could knock Oliver out like a sleeping draft.

We sat round the conservatory table, well supplied with alcohol and discussed my son's future. Now he was ten we had to decide on his continued education.

We went through various scenarios, then a thoughtful Bill came up with the idea of his moving in with them during term time and attending Alec's *alma mater* at Canterbury School.

Although her face didn't move a muscle, I knew Janet was not happy about it. Her fingers tightened slightly round her Scotch and soda and the liquid swung almost imperceptibly to one side.

"He might not want to do that," she said, knowing with a sinking heart he'd be delighted.

She turned to Alec, thinking he wouldn't want to be parted from his beloved son. We exchanged the briefest of glances and she knew her goose was well and truly cooked, but she went on anyway:

"What're your thoughts, Alec? You know the school better than the rest of us. Do you think Oliver would fit in?"

'Fit in' and not 'be happy'?

Her son rubbed his chin, thoughtfully.

"Well…," he considered. "He's very keen on baseball and games generally which they encourage, and if anyone can make him buckle down to his academic lessons, it'll be the masters there. They're not above using the paddle from time to time."

He suddenly realized the import of his statement.

"Oh… don't worry. There's no cruelty in the spanking. In any case, not many need it twice."

Far from being worried, I'd have given anything to be a fly on the wall. It must have shown in my face because Janet nudged me under the table. Fortunately, the two men were observing each other.

When Janet and I sat in the garden half an hour later, we clearly were looking at this from opposing directions. She was as white as a sheet. I was so relieved by the prospect before us, for a moment I was bereft of speech. In the absence of conversation, I lit us both a cigarette.

"I'll kill Bill for saying that without asking me," she seethed.

Oliver's response surprised me. He put up no argument at all. He liked the idea of living with his Grandpa. He asked if he and Uncle Duncan would take him to the shooting range sometimes at weekends, or better still onto the reserve to shoot turkey or pheasants. I saw Bill wince, remembering that poor little minnow Oliver'd thrown to the ground when he'd been snorkeling in the lake.

Both Alec and I felt distinctly uncomfortable once Oliver had gone. We'd finally have to admit, with only the two of us for company, our marriage had been a monumental mistake.

I foresaw me spending some extended time in California. Alec foresaw himself spending extended hours at work with Freddie Freeman. I don't know which of us was more delighted. In any case, the following morning we actually smiled, and he kissed my cheek.

I helped Janet prepare a little birthday tea in the garden. There were no children present, but Uncle Duncan came over from his farm at Elm Reach, and he and Bill played cops and robbers with Oliver round the trees, while Janet and I sipped tea.

True to form, Oliver was unimpressed by any of his gifts. We'd gone to infinite time and trouble, not to mention expense, to buy him a spectacular train-set with points, stations, platforms and remote control. It even had little trees and figures. But it was large, so we'd had to put it in one of the guest rooms at home and hope to excite his imagination with some large photographs Alec had made. That apparently, was tantamount to a spanking.

From Granny and Grandpa Maxwell, he had brand-new baseball gear of the very best quality, but he already had some, he said.

Then he was put out that he only had one set of grandparents while everyone else had two.

I didn't care one way or the other whether he had a happy birthday, and by the look on their faces, neither did Bill or Janet. Even Alec looked a bit put out.

Duncan went home later that afternoon, and so did we the following day. The relief was plainly apparent on my in-law's faces. At what point would Bill be regretting his generosity? Perhaps the thought had begun to sink in already. Janet was still grim-faced.

I hugged them both, promising to call when we got back

It was one of those days of brilliant color peculiar to Connecticut. The trees were gold and green and fields stretched, pitted and dimpled to the horizon on both sides of the highway.

In our individual ways, the visit had cheered us up. Oliver even hummed, of all things, 'Someday my Prince will Come' and mostly in tune.

He spent the rest of the journey napping and intermittently grilling his father about Canterbury. The way Alec described it, it was Luna Park with the occasional spanking. Boy, was his son in for a shock! I smiled peacefully to myself.

I left Alec to write his letter to the school, and Oliver to hopefully drown in the lake, and escaped to San Clemente. I really hadn't appreciated to that point what the purpose of a second home was, but I sure had learned.

I hadn't contacted Tina to let her know I'd be coming, so naturally she was a gibbering wreck when I banged on the door, which was easier than scrabbling about in the bottom of my purse for my keys.

I marched past her. I'd had enough of a journey to care much about her feelings.

"Dammit, Tina. I didn't let you know I was coming so I'll have to suffer your jeans. Put that apron away - it looks ridiculous. Fetch me a gin and tonic – make it strong, plenty of ice - then ring the rest of them and tell them they'll be needed for a couple of weeks.

But she only caught the gist as she'd dashed out to drag the covers off the terrace furniture. I helped her before she fainted from fright.

"Gin and tonic, Tina," I ordered, uncovering the last chair. She disappeared at a run.

What the hell was so scary about me? I'd never yelled at her or spoken to her in anything other than a professional manner as yet. I'd sit her down and try to get to the bottom of it…. sometime. Perhaps a little alcohol might oil the wheels.

She brought my g&t. I put my feet up, took a good slurp and rolled an ice-cube round my mouth. Oh, it was so good to be here. I strolled to the terrace rail. I was too far away to hear the surf, but I could imagine it's pounding.

The next morning was a beautiful October day, fine and clear. I showered, changed, and took a walk into town to shake off the indolence of hours on a plane. I even ran a few yards down the Ocean Walk before buying chicken and fries to-go and strolling down the pier. Freedom!

Walking back up the drive was not as easy as walking down. I had to stop every so often to catch my breath, but it gave me the chance to check out the hydrangeas still flowering along the way. The gardener had done a splendid job. The flowers grew in a cascade of toning colors just touching the top of the retaining walls all the way to the house door.

At the top, I stood back to examine my home. I was impressed with me. I'd done a great job. One thing was missing. There was a neat little space to the left of the door just right for a name plate, but I didn't have a name. I had no ideas at all.

I was alone. What now? Slowly my bright mood began to drift into despondency. I had a husband who annoyed me, a son I couldn't stand the sight of. My little girl and the love of my life were never coming back.

I had another couple of days of napping in the sun reading the occasional copy of Life Magazine and drinking far too many cocktails. All the things which caused stresses and strains in my life were half a continent away, but I couldn't make them go completely.

Alec called to say he'd written off to the school and was awaiting their reply. I could tell he was annoyed at having to suffer even more than usual of his beloved son. Rods for backs.

I took another slurp of my gin and tried to care. The Windham housekeeper had quit after a few days of suffering Oliver on her own while Alec was at work, and he wanted to know what to do. I told him to call his mother. She was the expert on staff.

"'Bye, Alec. Take care of yourself."

I sat outside on the doorsteps, a bit woozy.

There were fireflies beyond the edging stones amongst the stems of the bushes. Their flickering and dancing were making me cross-eyed. I pulled myself upright against the door jamb and again saw that tantalizing little space just crying out for a name.

I looked down at my empty glass and snapped my fingers – I had it – gin sling. I'd call it 'Ginsling House'. I'd order a slate plaque in the morning if I remembered. Strangely enough, I did.

It was probably as well that Janet turned up the following day. I was breakfasting on a nice healthy orange juice-based Buck's Fizz and ending it on gin. What happened between was anybody's guess.

Fortunately, I'd not bothered going out.

I can only assume Tina and Tommy cleared up after I'd lurched to bed.

Janet took one look at me and put on the coffee herself – double strength. Then she put me in the shower and turned it on cold. She didn't give a damn how I hollered.

She dried me, threw my robe at me and ordered me to drink the coffee.

"Och Aye, Mom," I said sheepishly.

"Don't you Mom me, you stupid brat. If I ever see you in that state again, I'll leave and never come back."

That sobered me up more than the cold shower.

I started to cry. I'm not sure why. Self-pity was part of it I supposed, but also shame and absolutely zero self-respect. I was still smarting from walking away from Trina, and by extension Charlie.

Conversely my angel seemed nearer. I'd thought he'd go once he'd taken Trina. I didn't dream about him anymore, but he was there. I could feel him.

My mother-in-law sat with her arms around me until I pulled myself together.

"Talk!," she commanded.

It wasn't a long conversation and contained the words Oliver and Alec a lot. With minor additions of Charlie and Trina. Janet did her usual and sat and listened silently, completely expressionless.

"Seems to me you have two choices. Stay at Windham or go. Which will it be? I'll leave you to think about that for a while."

She left me alone on the terrace and went to make the lives of my servants hell. She was going to give Tina a heart attack, so I stirred myself to write a brief shopping list and sent her to the market out of the way.

"Where's your chauffeur?," Janet asked through the sliding door. "I need a word."

"Don't have one – don't need one." I said, remembering Lon.

"Of course you do. Who'll do your airport runs and clean your car?"

"I'll have the car valeted and take cabs," and as her expression turned mulish, I added: "Don't push it."

She went back inside, muttering. She wasn't used to being overruled, especially by some spoilt brat she's spent the best part of the day sobering up.

I did give careful consideration to what she said though and came to the conclusion I would try having my cake and eating it first and see what happened.

Oliver was still at Annandale. I think Janet was rather hoping if I was fulltime at Windham, I might relocate him to a private school nearer home. There was plenty of choice, one just ten miles up the road.

Not a cat in hell's chance.

Alec was at work most of the time in any case, which was fine by me. He was happy to leave Oliver with the help in the holidays – he'd found a woman who looked like a wrestler and who scared Oliver to death. So far, she'd lasted the course.

I'd have to take up that duty again which both of us would hate. Either he'd have to learn to behave or make some friends. Alternatively, I could buy him a boat with a slow leak.

Or I could simply live here at Ginsling House, but it would be a lonely existence. I'd done the Bridge thing. There was a great tennis club in San Clemente, but I'd feel odd going by myself. I could try night school – I quite fancied learning Spanish or filling in the gaps as I had in Marcia's library. But it would mean locating here on a permanent basis to make that work. Which I supposed was Janet's point.

I don't think she cared what I decided. She'd still prefer my company to those of the men in her life, so she'd support me either way.

It suddenly occurred to me this was a pivotal point in my life. Do I go forward as a reluctant wife and mother or go solo and risk being forever alone?

Janet came back and sat waiting for me to speak.

"There's a bloody big chicken clucking away in my ear, Janet. I'm scared to death of the implications either way."

"This can only be your decision, Grace," she said, which was about the last thing I wanted to hear. "It's your life. Only you can make that choice. But for what it's worth, you have my sympathy."

I didn't say it's not worth a lot, but I thought it.

In the end, I did chicken out. I decided to let things chug along. The real problem was I loved both my houses. Windham was my home and San Clemente was where I went when I couldn't stand my home a moment longer. It should have been about the people, but it wasn't – it was a pure bricks and mortar matter.

Term was still in full swing, so Oliver was at school. He seemed to be doing okay – that is to say, he hadn't been expelled yet.

'Canterbury' had an Olympic sized swimming pool and full-sized football and baseball pitches which might have had a lot to do with it. I was dreading school open day when I discovered his academic prowess. Perhaps I could find a way of sloping off to San Clemente and leaving Alec to deal with that. I had no doubt at all he was having the same thought about me.

I hadn't seen Evie in an age. We were real rovers now – Janet from Connecticut, Evie from Nevada and me from Illinois. It was nice to have a fourth place to connect.

I called Evie, so a couple of days later, with Janet we donned our swimsuits under our clothes, rammed towels and sun block in beach bags and walked, lighthearted, to spend some time on the beach. I'm not a beach babe, but it was just so great to spend a day with people whose company I enjoyed.

We stuck to the 'buckets and spades' side of the pier. The other side with the surf was full of ex-GIs in shorts showing off on boards, for the benefit of giggly girls in swimsuits on the beach.

How I envied those girls. At their age I was aboard a filthy boat riding into New York harbor, then scrubbing someone else's house to keep body and soul together. I didn't even know beaches like that existed. Well, thanks to the floor-scrubbing, I got here in the end.

Janet, Evie and I enjoyed each other's company intermittently over the next few years, usually at Windham.

Alec was always at work, and I didn't visit him there because of his colleague Freddie Freeman. Having made repeated passes behind Alec's back, and being repulsed in no uncertain terms, he asked me if I was a Lesbian, the arrogant bastard - I could only assume he had suicidal tendencies.

I never went again, and if Alec found that odd, he was too busy or too disinterested to notice.

Janet absented herself from Annandale when she could. Duncan and Bill had begun taking Oliver to the shooting range. Bill said he was becoming very good. He joined the gun club at school, where the team competed at State level. His only fault seemed to be, once they had finished, he was lazy about cleaning his firearm before putting it away.

At school, only half of the lesson was actual shooting, the rest was tuition on the technique, care and maintenance of firearms, with special attention paid to safety and their history in the opening up of the American continent – the last bit he wasn't too bothered about.

But there was a good spin-off from this interest. In order to excel, he'd to know some physics and math and enough English to write good reports. To give him his due, he did settle down and put in some effort.

I have to admit in my heart of hearts, I was very nervous about giving him a gun. Alec thought it would teach him responsibility and that he would grow out of his childish behavior. I was dubious.

For his seventeenth birthday, we bought him a brand-new Buick Roadmaster – bright and shiny sea-green. He loved it and would spend hours tinkering under the hood. It was a real 'chick magnet' as he dubbed it.

He may not have been big on friends through his childhood, but once he discovered girls that was an entirely different matter. There was a new one on his arm for every social event. Most of them looked pretty clueless which was probably to their advantage.

Then he met Rachel Litton-Thomas. Her family as her name suggested were originally Georgia aristocrats, but her father had moved them to Los Angeles and owned a string of high-end car dealerships in better areas of the city. Rachel was an only child, a detail I suspect not lost on Oliver.

They actually met in LA, when Oliver was spending a few days at Ginsling House, which he'd renamed Pacific View for Rachel's benefit because he thought it was vulgar, which had been my intention of course. He didn't get to take down my name plaque though. She didn't seem to notice the discrepancy.

Of course, Oliver was always one with an eye for the main chance and could be very engaging if he chose. I could only think it was the money that attracted him, as Rachel was a frail nervous little thing who spoke with a put-on cultured accent. She had very pale, almost translucent skin and mousey hair, which she habitually wore in a French pleat. She didn't have a curve on her body.

I couldn't have imagined him engaging her attention with guns and cars. He on the other hand asked subtle questions about her father until she began to notice, then he stopped abruptly.

I watched mesmerized as their courtship progressed.

He'd been reading up. He bought her corsages of gardenias and bouquets of roses and freesia. He learned she liked Emily Dickinson poems – *lovely, death and depression* – and bought her a complete leather-bound volume of her works. In later years I had Emily Dickinson and Rachel inseparable in my mind.

On the other hand, Oliver had grown into a handsome lad. His love of sport gave him a natural, year-round tan which complimented his sparkling blue Crawford eyes and fine blond hair. He had great dress sense and usually went for expensive smart-casual. Pity he was a 'whited wall'. Inside was not so rosy.

He and Rachel made the most unlikely couple – together they made one whole person. She drab and cultured, he confident and sporty. She could read and write – he could run fast.

Chapter Twenty-nine

Murder Most Foul and a Puzzle for Grace

Oliver spent some time crisscrossing the country with his shooting competitions, and by the age of seventeen had gone as far as he could at junior and intermediate levels.

When he left school he graduated but only just. He took what he could from the curriculum to help with his guns but, unless Walt Whitman made rifles, he had no interest.

My son chose to move back to Windham, which meant he could join the National Rifle Association in Chicago, which was the controlling body for the whole of north America.

The Association had its own very exclusive private college, but I was secretly doubtful he would be accepted. These things seem to work not on 'what you know', but 'who you know'. Competitive shooting was very cliquey.

'The Senator's son scored a perfect round twice at the last outing. What a great young man. He'll make a splendid politician. Just like his father'.

In an effort to encourage Oliver's new-found ambitions, Alec had a cabin built for him in the garden, where he had a measure of privacy. He pleased Oliver by insisting only one key be cut so he could truly claim it as his own domain.

Alec installed a secure cabinet for Oliver's guns, of which he now had quite a collection. He made an effort to learn what he could of his son's interest, and when Oliver got bored, offered to go out with him to a nearby reserve.

"Let's go get Mom some duck for the freezer," he would say.

These excursions got to be quite a common occurrence, while he waited for the result of his application to come through for the NRA.

Father and son seemed drawn together by a perceived common interest.

Of course, conversely, Mom was pushed out. So, mother spent more time at Ginsling. Which upset Mom not at all.

I invited Evie over to San Clemente, and we sat chewing the fat on the terrace for a couple of days. When we got bored, we decided a day shopping in Los Angeles might be fun.

I showed her the little boutique where I had bought that appalling dining table and chairs. Then we trawled the fashion stores until we were exhausted.

It seemed like a good idea to have a light meal at a little bistro I knew, to rest up before we headed back home. We were tucking into salad and a glass of wine when I thought I saw a familiar face across the street.

"Isn't that Oliver?" said Evie who had noticed him at the same time.

"Yes, and he's with Rachel. I don't keep tabs on him, but I thought he was at Windham with his Dad this weekend. He must be staying at the Thomas's. Litton-Thomas's should have a stately home near London rather than a condo in the suburbs of Los Angeles."

Before I could stop her, Evie was on the sidewalk outside the restaurant, waving her arms in the air as if she was guiding a Hellcat onto a carrier deck.

"Hey! Oliver – over here! Come and have lunch with your mom and me! My treat."

I hid my face behind my hand and prayed he'd go away. He did. Oh what a relief. Evie came back looking a bit put out.

"I could swear he saw me, but he just took his girl's arm and walked away. How odd."

"Not odd at all. I'm not his favorite social companion. No loss – come on, let's go home."

It was Alec's turn to call me. We were both so bored by the prospect we'd to take it in turns. When he hadn't answered or returned my calls by the following day, I started to get annoyed.

I rang Janet to see if he was there, but she hadn't seen him either. I have to say she was a better mother than I was a wife. She worried.

"You know what he's like Janet – he goes on these work splurges and forgets his own name. I'll call Freddie the Fruitcake and see if he's heard from him."

But Freddie hadn't heard from him either, which *was* remarkable.

It must have played on Janet's mind because she caught the next convenient flight to O'Hare, and eventually did find her son.

She rang me at Ginsling, but for a good minute there was no sound but police and ambulance sirens. Then a choked voice said:

"Alec's on his way to hospital, Grace. He fell in Oliver's cabin and hit his head on the cabinet. Grace, there was just so much blood.... blood everywhere."

She began to sob.

"I could see his legs on the floor through the bench window, but I couldn't get in... the door was locked, and the window wouldn't break... I couldn't find a stone big enough... I'm sorry Grace... I'm so sorry. I did call the ambulance. He was still alive. I called the ambulance, Grace. No... no I didn't – one of the servants did, I think.... I think that's right. Is that right?"

She spoke faster and faster and her voice ended in a screech.

"What do you want to do, Janet?," I asked, striving for calm. "I'll be there as fast as I can. Stay there if you like, but if you're too freaked, go home."

She made a concerted effort - this was her son, and she didn't know what was going on. But Janet had more strength of character than anyone I ever knew.

"I'll go to the hospital. He's bad, darling. The paramedics would say nothing. They just dressed his head wound and put him on a drip before they left. They left so fast, Grace. They were driving with the sirens going. They forgot me," she ended pathetically.

"Which hospital is it? I'll meet you there as fast as possible."

I told Evie what had happened and went to pack a bag.

It took me nearly eight hours to get to Chicago. The flight was only four, but I'd a long wait before I could get on a plane. An ideal husband Alec wasn't, but I didn't want to see him hurt.

I enquired as to his whereabouts from an emotionless hospital receptionist who asked if I was family.

"I'm his wife," I said, waving my driver's license under her nose.

I dropped my bag on the floor next to her desk and hurtled up the stairs rather than wait for an elevator.

Janet was sitting on a chair in the corridor waiting room. She leapt to her feet and threw herself into my arms.

"He was recovering. Then the doctor told me he had developed a swelling on the brain, and they took him for emergency surgery. Grace, Gracie…. he's been in there for four hours. No one will tell me anything. I see nurses come and go at a rush, but they pass so quickly. Something must be badly wrong."

I needed to know more, so I tackled the theatre administrator at her desk.

"I'm Alec Maxwell's wife. I understand he's in surgery. I've just flown in from Los Angeles. His mother is here, and no-one will tell her anything. Why not?"

I rapped on her desktop, worry making me aggressive.

"I'm afraid I can tell you nothing Mrs. Maxwell, until he comes out of surgery. You'll have to wait, I'm afraid. I'll have one of the nurses fetch you some coffee."

Although I knew she could do nothing, it didn't stop me being rude.

"I don't want any goddamn coffee – I want to know when he'll be out of surgery and, more important, how he is."

She shrugged and held up her hands. She must have seen this situation a hundred times. I took a deep breath and calmed down. This approach would get me nowhere.

"I apologize Miss….," I said, looking for her name badge, "… Nurse Miller. I've had a very stressful journey and my mother-in-law is beside herself with worry. Thank you. We'd both appreciate the coffee."

We hadn't even got our drink before we were told Alec was dead.

I'd to leave Janet in the care of a young nurse when I was summoned to the surgeon's office. He took a good half hour to arrive, during which time I had smoked half a pack of Marlboro and a cloud like a London fog engulfed the room.

Alec had had a seizure caused by shock and loss of blood. They hadn't been able to resuscitate him. Had he been admitted a few hours earlier, it might have been different.

"Do you know how long the accident happened before he was admitted?"

I struggled to maintain some dignity, while I choked on my words.

"Quite some time before he was found. It's hard to be exact. In addition to the blow to the head, he also had internal injuries which are very difficult to assess."

"I must see my mother-in-law – she's distraught and there are family members I need to speak to. I'm sorry – I'm not taking this in at all."

I felt so disorientated – nothing seemed to be making sense. Alec? No… impossible. There must be some mistake. Yet here I was sitting in a surgeons office in a hospital in Chicago so there could be no question. And shit – I had to face Janet!"

"Take Mrs. Maxwell home and I'll have my surgical assistant call you later. We don't have the full facts yet in any case."

When I returned to the waiting room to collect Janet, a young nurse had given her a shot to calm her nerves and she'd managed to pull herself together.

She'd then made the questionable decision not to call Bill with the news, but to travel home and break it to him as gently as she could, face to face. That meant the best part of a day! Poor Janet. Her reaction reminded me of battle fatigue in the war – given the circumstances, it seemed totally illogical.

When she'd first heard of Alec's condition, she'd driven to the hospital in my car, so I left her at the airport on my way back. I offered to sit with her until her flight was called, but she refused saying she'd appreciate a little time to herself. Nevertheless, I watched her from a distance in case she needed me.

I drove home alone, pretty fearful of what I'd find.

By the time I got there, The cabin had been cordoned off by the police. I wasn't allowed through the tape because they were still examining the scene. I could see what looked like oceans of blood and the bench where Oliver cleaned and maintained his guns. The door lock was broken, and the wood splintered down the side, I assumed where the police or the paramedics had broken it in.

There were two guns on the worktop, so I assumed he must have been out shooting with his dad. One of them was partly disassembled, as if in the process of being cleaned. The barrel of the second gun was on the bench, but its stock was laying on the floor in a puddle of blood. The cabinet door was ajar.

The police officer suggested I go and deal with my house staff. Probably to give me something to do and get me out of the way.

I told one of the maids to run up to Alec's room and fetch the camera from his bureau. Back at the cabin I gave the camera to the detective in charge, and asked him to take a couple of photos, so I could tell them if anything was missing. I couldn't shake the feeling that something was not quite right.

It just showed how much Oliver penetrated my consciousness. I hadn't thought to contact him since this catastrophe occurred, but I supposed he might be vaguely interested his father was dead.

I returned to the house to speak to the servants and explain what had happened.

"Does anyone know where Mr. Oliver is?" I asked, "He hasn't been informed yet."

They all adopted identical expressions of concern.

Richardson the gardener, took charge and answered for the whole staff.

"Last time I saw him Ma'am, was yesterday morning. He said he would be going to Los Angeles to visit Miss Rachel."

"Did any of you notice anything untoward in the garden or around the house in the early hours? The police will need to be informed." I told the assembled servants.

"No, Ma'am. Mr. Oliver and Dr. Maxwell went out to Threshfield Reserve shooting late the previous afternoon. I saw them pull into the drive on their return, just as I was leaving. I didn't see Dr. Maxwell again. But Mr. Oliver left, as I said, later the following morning.

Yes, Evie and I had seen them both from our restaurant table that afternoon.

It turned out Richardson had been right. I tracked Oliver down to Rachel's family home in Burbank. I rang and asked him to come home as his Dad had had an accident. He already knew his Dad was dead as he'd been informed by the LA police.

This was rock bottom even for Oliver.

"I knew you were at San Clemente," he said, "so I rang and got no reply – several times. The staff must have been out."

The last he added as if it was a reasonable explanation.

"So, you didn't ring Windham either? Even if I wasn't there, you could have left a message."

"Well, I'm sorry," he said, peevishly, "I don't have a crystal ball, so I didn't know Dad'd had an accident. I'd arranged to meet Rachel and Mr. Litton-Thomas. He's sponsoring a car at the Mexico Grand Prix, and he's asked me to go with him. You don't need me for anything, do you? I'll be back in plenty of time for the funeral if that's what you're worried about."

"Get your ass back here NOW!," I yelled down the phone.

He hung up.

That evening I took out the photos the policeman had taken for me and made large copies in Alec's darkroom.

It was possible it could have been a break-in I supposed, but compared to the contents of the house, the gun room was small potatoes. Any thief worth their salt would have known that. In any case why would a stranger go looking for something in a building resembling a garden shed?

I spread the photos over my bed. Oliver's favorite hunting rifle was still in the cabinet. I couldn't tell from the pieces which gun had been disassembled on the worktop but could clearly see the stock which was closest to the door. It had CHM burned into the wood so I figured it must be an old one from school.

I still hadn't figured out what it was about the photos which struck me as odd. I walked up and down the room. Nope. Nothing.

Perhaps if I ignored it the answer would come to me.

Once the autopsy had been completed, and the police had released Alec's body, I put arrangements for the funeral in the hands of a professional company. Evie offered to come and help with the catering and flowers. I was spent and so grateful to her.

The day before the service Janet, Bill and Duncan arrived. I had never been so relieved to see anyone in my life. I was so sad for Janet. Her skin was waxen and her hair seemed to have gone white overnight. She was leaning heavily on Bill's arm and Duncan was trailing after them like a lost dog.

I showed them to their rooms, and they were just out of the way before Oliver wafted in smelling of exhaust fumes. Not really, but that's how I thought of it at the time.

He threw his key ring on the hall table on the way in - I hated when he did that. It scratched the mirror surface. I snatched it up and dropped it into a drawer in the table. The keys were heavy so they trapped in the drawer as I shut it.

Why would they be so bulky? I ticked them off curiously.

His Windham keys were there – he didn't have the ones for Ginsling. There was a spare for my car which he'd borrowed and not bothered returning and the cabin key. There was a heavy rather ornate one I assumed belonged to Rachel's parents - I'd never seen it before. It must have been that which had trapped in the drawer.

His own car keys were missing so I assumed he'd left them with Rachel.

Meanwhile, Oliver was displaying his true colors before the entire family.

"Oh Mom… whatever shall we do? Dad was the mainstay of this family – what on earth will we do without him."

The two-faced bastard. He even had the nerve to wink at me when everyone's backs were turned.

There wasn't much to say about the funeral. The director asked if I'd like the casket open or closed. Not being overly keen on corpses I opted for closed.

As for the rest, it was a funeral – casket, flowers, pews, and soggy hankies. Oliver made a heart-rending eulogy which he read off the back of an envelope. When all this was over, he and I were finished.

My husband hadn't left a Will so his estate in its entirety came to me. I was gratified to notice Oliver's look of consternation when he realized. He'd never cared for my opinion before so I looked forward to making him squirm.

Alec was interred in a pretty little cemetery, north of Windham. It had many-colored rose bushes and neatly manicured lawns. Janet, who had remained resolutely stiff-backed throughout the service, wept openly at the graveside. I was glad she let go. She needed to.

I suppose it can't have helped that she'd held her one and only son in contempt for pretty much his entire life. He'd irritated the hell out of her, and guilt is a terrible thing. She looked at me sideways from time to time, but she avoided eye-contact. I'd go see her when all this was over. Perhaps she could spend a few days at Ginsling to rest and recuperate.

The Maxwell's left the morning after the funeral, glad I think to try for some peace. I hugged Janet and told her I'd be in touch in a few days when she'd had time to rest.

Oliver took a cab to the airport then went back to LA and Rachel.

So, apart from my staff, I was now alone. What a relief that was.

I fixed myself a drink than strolled down to the lake. Twilight is a time for specters. Alec perhaps – or perhaps Charlie and little Trina with their angel. In times of trouble, I often fancied I felt Charlie's presence. After all these years, and all that had happened between, my feelings and memories had never faded.

I was suddenly overcome with fatigue and wandered back indoors. A husband's funeral tends to make for a stressful day. I put my glass on the counter and went to my room.

Chapter Thirty

An Enigma Uncovered and a Staggering Revelation

Before I slept, I took a look at the photographs again.

Something not right…... not right. It was turning round and round in my head. There was something about this that wasn't right.

Then it clicked.

I flew downstairs and grabbed the keys from the hall table drawer and counted them off: Windham – front, back, conservatory. No Ginsling. My own car key, the unknown key and the cabin key…. THE CABIN KEY. That was it.

No one but Oliver had a key to the cabin – Alec had insisted he should feel the place was entirely his own, so there had only ever been one key.

And the paramedics had had to break the door down, so Oliver must have locked it himself. He was the only one who could. So, he must either be responsible or know who was.

But Evie and I had seen him in LA with Rachel the afternoon after Alec's death, so it couldn't have been him. Unless….

It was three o'clock in the morning in Windham, Illinois. There was only an hour's time difference with New York. I couldn't wake Janet up in the middle of the night although only she had the answers.

Eventually I could stand the suspense no longer and took the next flight to New York. Either that or bite my nails to the elbows in the meantime.

It was seven thirty when I arrived at Annandale. I'd watched the sunrise over the world's edge through a double layer of glass, while my foot tapped with agitation against the seat in front. Its occupant gave me a look to strip paint.

I had the cab drop me at the bottom of the drive and walked the rest of the way, but the house was still locked and shuttered. Either they weren't there – unlikely – or still sleeping.

I sat on the step for a while, then deliberately broke my promise to Janet and walked the half mile to sit with my daughter. My crocuses had proliferated, and now the grass about the headstone was studded with amethyst and gold.

Janet must have visited from time to time. The headstone was pristine and sun-dappled through the leaves of the sugar maple. A small bunch of freesias lay across her feet. It was one of those occasions I felt Charlie most strongly – so strongly that I patted my shoulder where his hand lay.

I walked away before my burden became too heavy to bear. The Apocalypse was about to come – I needed to summon all my strength.

It was near nine o'clock before I got back to the house. It was now fully astir, and my bag had been taken from the stoop.

Janet was sitting in the conservatory in her robe, sipping tea. There were slices of toast on the table, but they were untouched, as was a glass of orange juice.

The light had gone from this erstwhile optimistic, feisty woman. She looked at me with weary eyes.

"Hello, darling Grace," she intoned. "Do come and sit with me."

She knocked some ash from her cigarette onto the floor. Damn, things were bad.

"Bill is with Duncan," she said, apropos nothing at all.

I adopted a faux cheeriness before we both sank into a pit of despond.

"Come on. You get dressed and we'll have lunch at that little Italian restaurant in Danbury."

I could have bitten my tongue off – how could I be so stupid. That was Alec's favorite restaurant. He took me there on our first date. I could say nothing without making things worse, so I changed the subject.

"Let's go take a walk – it's such a lovely day. The fresh air will do you good."

We strolled along faint paths through forest glades. The only sounds were birdsong and the occasional snap of a disturbed twig. It was balm to the soul.

Janet seemed to rally. Her steps quickened and she looked about her with renewed interest. Too bad I was going to knock that on the head with a vengeance.

"Let's go back now," I said after an hour or so. "I have some questions to ask you."

She took my arm and we strolled back the way we had come in silence. The sun seemed less bright as we neared the house.

"Dora…," she yelled as we entered. "Put the big decanter of brandy from the dining room and a couple of glasses in the sitting room. Ice too."

Where to begin?

"I'm sorry to have to raise this subject again, but do you recall what time it was when you discovered Alec at Windham?"

She jumped at the unexpectedness of the question and gazed out of the window frowning.

"I guess it must have been about eleven o'clock in the morning. My flight got in at ten. Clearing the airport and driving down will have taken about an hour – perhaps a little more. Why do you ask?"

How to tell her her grandson may have murdered her son?

"I have a theory to put to you," I began. "I beg you to please prove me wrong because the alternative is …. well, frankly, terrifying."

Janet knew I wasn't given to hyperbole, so she sat up straight and the old intelligence reawakened in her eyes. She filled our glasses generously and dropped ice cubes into each.

"Go on," she said and gulped half a glass of brandy.

I went through the whole scenario I'd been working on on the flight over:

"I think it must have been Oliver who was responsible for Alec's death.

"According to the surgeon, Alec must have been hurt some hours before you found him, which given the time zone difference between Chicago and Los Angeles meant Oliver could still have done the deed and been in LA well before Evie and I saw him around four o'clock.

"The police or ambulance personnel had had to break down the cabin door to reach Alec – it was knocked off its hinges inwards, and the wood splintered all the way down the side of the lock which meant it must have been secured from the outside. Oliver had the only key as you know and it was on the key-ring he left on the table at Windham – he obviously hadn't lost it.

She excused herself and spent nearly half-an-hour walking aimlessly round the garden. I watched her from the window.

When she returned, she lowered herself thoughtfully onto the sofa, then threw up her hands in despair.

"Nothing else fits. There's no other way to construe it unless he'd lost the key, which he clearly hadn't. Are you absolutely sure of all your facts? There can be no doubt?"

By way of confirmation, I took the keys from my purse and explained each one to her.

"How could he have been so stupid? He's left us with no alternative but to report him to the authorities," she sighed

"Well, there is a route we could take which might work. I need to make a number of visits in Danbury – but that will wait for another day. You look exhausted."

I saw her to bed and pulled the drapes. Whether she slept or not I didn't know.

A couple of days later she said she had something to show me. She was quite firm about it as if she had given the matter some careful consideration.

I was surprised to be retracing my steps to the garden of rest where Trina lay because Janet had been so adamant I should stay away.

But instead of stopping to look at my baby's grave, she walked past into the quaint little chapel nearby. I knew it was always open, but I had never thought to go in before. It was built of buttery limestone and had a mosaic floor of blues and white. There was a small stained-glass window – not the ancient stained glass of England, but from its Art Nouveau style, perhaps fifty years old.

There was a small altar under the window which Janet pushed back to reveal a carved slab of the same limestone. On it were carved the words:

Here lie the remains of Isobel Scott McClean

Dearly beloved daughter of Andrew McClean and Janet Crawford

May the Angel of Light guard and guide you, sweet soul.

1910 – 1912

I looked at her open-mouthed.

"No one on earth but you and I know about this. I beg you not to share it with a soul. Even Andrew doesn't know.

I had my baby, Isobel, cremated in secret and fetched her with me from Scotland – I just couldn't leave her. You are the only person I have ever felt might understand an empty grave."

She leaned over and rested her head briefly against my shoulder, then pulled the habitual handkerchief from her sleeve and blew her nose loudly. Together we pulled the altar back into place.

With some trepidation she continued:

"Now I've finally told you, would you have Trina placed beside Bella? It's stupid I know. They both died long ago, but I'd feel it a comfort to know my little Bella had a companion. And it's more secluded here than outside."

For the first time ever, it occurred to me Janet must now be in her seventies – an old lady. Was she making sure her little daughter was taken care of once she was gone? I took a sideways glance. It was as if a weight had been lifted from her shoulders. Perhaps for her, this wasn't about Oliver at all.

We walked hand-in-hand to Trina's resting place and she took note of the inscription, seemingly for the first time although she'd visited often.

"Oh!," she exclaimed in surprise. "Trina has an angel too? Have you seen him?"

Chapter Thirty-one

Oliver Gets his Comeuppance

It took several more weeks for the police to wrap up their enquiries. I found out nothing happened quickly at the CPD. Meanwhile the blood-soaked cabin lay cordoned off in my garden.

Their final conclusion was Alec had been murdered 'by person or persons unknown'. I said an inward prayer for patience – even Marcia, clued up on Agatha Christy could have had a crack at this one.

Once I'd accounted for my own whereabouts, I gave Oliver his alibi, and told the police a friend and I had seen him in Los Angeles at the time of the murder. I intended doling out my own justice. Not only for Alec but for me and Janet.

After that, I didn't want to see him until I had everything in place. Besides, the longer I left it, the more off-guard he would be. How could a mother have such hatred for her only living child? To me he was the anti-Christ and justice had become a Crusade.

I went to see my attorney in Danbury. The Mr. Moffat who had dealt with Marcia's Will was long dead. His grandson, Mr. Johnson, had had charge of my affairs for quite some time now.

I asked him to scrutinize a letter Janet and I had put together to ensure our own safety, and to put it in legal terms.

The gist of the document was, should anything untoward happen to me or Janet – indeed, any of Oliver's family –

the police were to be notified of his actions regarding his father's death – a separate sealed envelope addressed to the CPD was included which gave details.

I also left the keys with Mr. Johnson for safekeeping and stamped my foot in annoyance that I hadn't thought to unscrew the matching lock from the cabin door.

Mr. Johnson informed me the work would be finished by the end of the week. I asked for two copies sealed with wax, one marked 'For the Personal Attention of Mr. Oliver Harper Maxwell – Private and Confidential' with a notarized copy for his signature. The other I asked him to mark 'Personal Documents for the Exclusive Access of Mrs. Grace Ellen Harper Maxwell and Mrs. Janet Crawford Maxwell' signed by the pair of us.

I asked for ours to be kept locked away in his safe together with the keys.

I took Oliver's document and its copy with me.

Then I visited the bank next door, where were kept two security boxes containing my jewels and twenty million dollars in cash. All my dealings had been by mail since I moved from Annandale, but I had the two security box keys and an authorization document signed by myself and the manager's predecessor.

"I would like you to make out a banker's draft for the sum of one million dollars, payable to Mr. Oliver Harper Maxwell."

The bank manager's eyes nearly popped out of his head. This was Danbury. Most of his mundane day to day business would be savings and current accounts with the occasional mortgage.

"I will deposit the amount in my account today for you to draw on."

I moved a million bucks, plus extra to finish fixing up Windham, to my account.

Since I'd given him his alibi, Oliver thought he had us over a barrel and he'd gotten away with it. He'd never mentioned the lost keys, but my housekeeper said he'd been back and seemed to be searching for something. He'd left again within a couple of hours.

It was easy to get Oliver to Annandale. Even after all that had happened, the promise of a weekend's shooting with his grandfather and Uncle Duncan was good bait. Putting my father-in-law and his brother within a hundred miles of Oliver with a gun, scared the hell out of me, but Janet was more sanguine. I even got the impression she was enjoying this. Perhaps revenge would be sweet for her too.

Our meeting with Oliver took place in Bill's home office. I sat behind the desk with a small bow-backed chair, purposely sized and positioned opposite, to put his eyelevel below my own.

Janet sat behind me, pokerfaced.

It was only when Bill showed him into the room, he realized there was anything untoward. Bill left, closing the door softly behind him.

"Good day, Mama. And how are you today? Looking quite well, if I may say so. That particular shade of apricot suits you."

If he was suspicious, he didn't show it.

"Sit down, Oliver," I said without preamble. He took out his pocketknife and began paring his nails with a secret little smile on his handsome face.

"Dora – fetch the brandy," ordered Janet.

"I'd prefer a Californian sherry if you have such a thing."

"Fetch Sherry too." And turning to Oliver said. "It's from Spain. Hope it suits."

I'd cleared the desktop and put Oliver's letter and bankers' draft in the pen drawer.

Dora entered with the drinks. Janet gave her and the rest of the staff the day off.

Oliver helped himself to the sherry without pouring for his grandmother and me. Janet put that straight, then sat back down in her chair, observing Oliver over the top of her glass. He was beginning to look a bit uncomfortable. I allowed the silence to stretch out into a battle of wills. He lost.

"Well ladies, what can I help you with?"

"On the contrary Oliver, it's what we can help *you* with." I withdrew the parchment envelope with its crimson seal from the drawer and slid it across the polished tabletop. His name was clearly written in brown copperplate script on its front.

"It's your copy of a contract. You needn't open it. This is an authorized facsimile for your signature," I said.

He took the copy and read it twice, perhaps three times with increasing discomfort, then looked us both up and down.

"Well? So, what does this prove?" He held my eye arrogantly. "All it says is my Dad died and I knew about it. You have no way of proving I was there at the time of his death."

Janet chortled into her drink.

"That so? Lost something?," asked his grandmother, then searched through her purse and slapped a photograph down beside the letter.

"Recognize these, boy?"

It was a picture of the keys, the offending cabin key prominently displayed.

"I'm not stupid enough to have brought them with me. They're lodged with my attorney," I told him.

Oliver's complexion had become ashen. He knew the significance of the single key and began to pick at his fingers in barely suppressed agitation. Janet had taught me well. I picked up on the small signs. Sight, demeanor and a very slight body odor.

I was not proud of the fact that both his grandmother and I so much wanted his fall from grace.

Looking at us, he must have known we had him at a disadvantage.

"We have a proposition for you. I suggest you consider it carefully before making a decision."

I took the bankers' draft from the drawer and placed it facing him, beside the letter and its copy – and of course the photograph. His vivid blue eyes were wide with shock.

"You may have this but there is a price," I said, tapping the banker's draft. It's yours, no strings – on the one condition you leave and never return. Never, Oliver. You are not to set eyes on me, your grandmother and grandfather and Uncle Duncan ever again. You will be removed from your family inheritance. The break will be total, do you understand me?"

He casually leaned back in his chair and scrutinized me over steepled fingertips. Then said in a quietly threatening voice:

"I fail to see what you have left me to consider. You know I am responsible for my father's death, and you will either turn me in or pay me off. Not very maternal of either of you."

"I would hardly say knocking your old man off was filial, would you, dear boy?," said Janet.

"Got me there, Granny," he sneered. "But you have to agree he was such a fool. How could you respect someone it was always so easy to manipulate? Momma there was a much worthier opponent."

"Just out of interest, why did you do it, anyway?," I said, "Not that at this stage it makes much difference, but I am curious as to why my husband is lying in a box in Illinois. I'm sure your Grandmother would like to know too."

"He was such a pedantic fool. He was insisting I clean my gun before putting it back in the cabinet and I hadn't time. I'd to catch a plane to LA. Geoff and I had some business to conclude. I gave him a shove and he fell and hit his head. That's all."

Well, that was a goddam lie! Even I could see Alec had been bashed over the head with the gun stock.

I regarded him thoughtfully, head on one side. How could this be? He was a very beautiful young man, in the way of the Maxwells – fine white-blond hair with a skin which tanned at the first touch of sun. His eyes were bluer than the Pacific Ocean. He could be urbane – charming, in fact. He had a good education and more money than he knew what to do with, thanks to Alec.

Perhaps he'd decided his future lay with Geoffrey Litton-Thomas, who he figured was probably better off.

While Geoffrey owned a string of car dealerships, and Oliver's grandparents were of generous means, he had always assumed I was the poor relation, as he'd never been able to figure out who my parents were.

So, naturally he'd thought it was Maxwell money which had bought the houses at Windham and San Clemente. I couldn't suppress a small grin.

"We shall have to see what happens with Papa's Will then, won't we? I'm sure he won't have left me wanting. After all, I'm his only child," he said, but despite his bravado he knew he was grasping at straws. He already knew there was no Will.

That didn't stop my sheer delight in confirming the fact.

"Sadly for you Oliver, your father left no Will, so as his legal spouse everything comes to me."

No need to tell him the deeds to both houses were in my name as well.

He scribbled his signature to the copy of the contract, snatched up the money and his own document, and left in a fury, thwarted at every turn.

"Well, that went well," said Janet.

Chapter Thirty-two
Crime Scene and a Visit Home

I left Janet looking considerably more cheerful than I'd found her. Beats me why – she'd just lost a grandson as well as a son but perhaps she just thought justice had been served and I hadn't killed my son in retaliation.

I don't know if she ever told Bill and Duncan what had happened, but I do know neither ever questioned Oliver's absence.

I went back to Windham the following week. I'd work to do.

The first major job was getting rid of that fucking cabin!

The police had taken down all their barriers and I manage to wrench away the temporary planking they put up as security. The inside had been thoroughly scoured and the guns removed to 'a place of safety' where they were being examined and would be returned 'in due course'. This may be judged in terms of months I supposed, since I'd heard nothing.

In fact, all traces of Alec, and by default Oliver, had been thoroughly excised. I called in a firm of builders to disassemble the building and dig up its foundations. I wanted it completely obliterated.

Throughout all their disorientation I had paid the staff, so they were all there except for a parlor maid who had moved away to get married. I was gratified that their loyalty appeared to have been to me, rather than Alec and

Oliver. Or perhaps it was just money for old rope, as the saying goes.

Anyway, I was back now so there was a lot of 'chopchopping' and the return of discipline. I had them turn the place out completely, and stripped Oliver's room right down to the plaster.

As I could never bear to go in it myself, I gave it over to the servants for a small parlor. I gave them a budget and let them furnish and decorate it themselves.

Richardson and his lad had kept the garden beautiful in my absence. My rhododendrons had been lovingly cared for and were in profusion. The roses had been pruned and had blossomed, darkening the tunnel between the house and the beach.

It must have been about a week later and still undecided, I walked to the hidden corner of the garden which had housed the cabin. After the builders had completed their work, Richardson had extended the lawn and left a border ready for planting.

"I didn't quite know what to do with it Mrs. Maxwell, but I thought perhaps you would like it tidied at least."

He was a good man. He didn't know the details of what had happened and was too considerate to pry.

"When you have a little time, I would appreciate a report on exactly what has happened in the grounds since I've been away. Leave nothing out."

"Yes, Ma'am."

He walked away with his arm round the shoulders of his lad who seemed to have grown two feet in my absence. He'd need a man's wage soon or I would have to let him go.

I did some of my best thinking at the lakeside, so I went to the shore, pulled up a lounger and dabbled my toes in the icy water.

After careful consideration I decided to plant a Japanese maple in the spot where the cabin had stood. I thought perhaps it might have reminded Alec of the larger Connecticut trees which surrounded Annandale.

The first sapling the gardener planted withered and died within a month, which was disturbing and made me shiver. I told him to buy a more mature plant, which fortunately took well.

The following morning my gardener handed in his report. It was scrawled in pencil and the pages had smudges of earth on them.

He'd had the remains of the wooden building stacked at the bottom of the garden near his compost heap, until he learned what I wanted to do with it. I told him to burn it.

Then I'd had enough. I'd got rid of anything which might disturb her, so I asked Janet if she would like to visit. Understandably she declined but had another suggestion which came as something of a surprise. She thought she might like to visit Scotland, which would probably be her last chance. Would I like to come? We could visit Halifax as well if I wanted. It wasn't that far from the Scottish border.

I wasn't too taken with the Halifax idea, but I thought it might be fun watching her walk down Memory Lane. A cousin still owned the manor near Annan she'd grown up in.

She wanted to go with me Janet said, as the alternative was going with Bill, and she'd had enough of the men in her family for a while.

We flew into Prestwick airport with its new terminal, picked up a hire car and drove the couple of hours to Janet's childhood home. We passed impossibly green fields, neatly trimmed hedges, their rows still bright with meadowsweet. It was enchanting.

"How did you ever leave? It's so beautiful," I asked.

"Two words – Andrew McClean."

She didn't speak again until we neared our destination but gazed out of the window at the passing scenery. I wondered what memories were taking shape behind her blank expression. At one point I glanced across, and a single tear had rolled down her cheek.

What Janet described as a manor looked to me more like a stately home. But then what did I know? The nearest I'd come to a smart residence in my youth, was walking past Shibden Hall, and that was half the size of my holiday home in San Clemente.

In order to get to the house, we drove through a park of deer, grazing in small family groups on lush grass. The house itself was hardly Pemberley but was solidly square with a porch held aloft by Ionic columns with a flight of steps beneath. A lawn gently sloped from the carriage turning circle we pulled up in.

We were greeted warmly by the Crawfords, Janet's family who had the present tenure of the house. It comprised Jonathan St Claire Crawford and his wife Marianna and two small daughters, Mina and Araminta (Araminta St Claire Crawford? Poor child!) Seventeen-year-old son, Tim was in his final year at Dulwich College in London.

Despite the debilitating names, they appeared to be warm friendly people, much given to Tweed and lambswool. I could imagine Marianna striding across the fells holding a shepherd's crook, and Jonathan riding to hounds.

We were ushered upstairs, by oil-painted ranks of generations past, and given adjoining rooms with an antiquated bathroom across the hall.

The rooms had been Janet's nursery and bedroom when she was a child, and their walls had since been hung with what looked to be original Cicely Mary Barker fairy paintings. The beds had plush mattresses twice as deep as the ones I'd so admired at Marcia Hamilton's, and my window looked out over a small lawn, sheltered by an orchard of apple and cherry in full fruit.

I excused myself and told Janet I'd take a walk to give her time to catch up on family news.

Ruminant deer observed me with disinterest, before resuming their leisurely munching.

The day was one of those early autumn ones so beloved of Keats – warm and still, with the loud buzzing of bees in the flowers and golden sunlight.

On the other side of the woods, I looked out over gently swelling Border hills, transected by ancient dry-stone walls.

When I returned to the house, it was to clap my hands in delight. Marianna had set out on the lawn, the daintiest of garden teas. Janet smiled and continued to pour into the egg-shell cups and saucers.

"Now you know where I learned it," she said.

I was then put through the Crawford family joke and seated several yards from the table with cup in one hand and plate in the other.

Janet saw my dilemma and laughed loudly.

"She knows that one, Marianna. Think of something else!"

A few days of pleasant strolls and reminiscences later, Janet decided it was time we drove down to Halifax. I presumed after this pleasant interlude the contrast would be shocking, but she only said:

"You saw all our sheep out on the hills? My father sold the wool, not in Halifax but in a remote part of the West Riding not ten miles away - Hebden Bridge. Do you know it? What do you imagine paid for this lovely house and its grounds?"

I was surprised.

"I know Hebden well. My brothers and sisters and I used to walk to the woods there to pick bilberries in the summer."

Halifax was as depressing as ever, with smokestacks and soot encrusted buildings, just as I recalled.

The town was clearly wealthier than I remembered, when boys as young as twelve would be walking to work to the mills in ragged clothing scrubbed clean for pride by their mothers.

"Where did you live?," asked my friend. "Let's visit. We can stay in the car if you prefer."

It says something of the trust we had developed, that I took her to row after row of identical cobbled terraces just off Gibbet Street. They were still as black as I remembered but looked far smaller and more cramped. There were lines of washing slung from house to house across streets with no gardens, and the remains of privies in back yards.

I well-remembered the two bedrooms – mother and father in one, and children squashed together in the other, until the boys began to grow to manhood and were relegated to mattresses on the kitchen floor.

It was as far from Windham and San Clemente and their wide open spaces as to be on another planet.

Well, we'd come all this way, so I got out of the car and began to walk down Chapel Street where I'd grown up, standing outside number seventeen, my former home.

A woman in a headscarf pushed past me, excusing herself. She was much my age but grey-haired and pale. She could have been Addie for all I knew. It was just so depressing.

Janet said nothing when I got back in the car, but drove off, back the way we'd come. Once out of town, I broke the silence:

"Thanks for making me come. It was a salutary lesson to appreciate what I have."

"We all need pulling up short from time to time. God and his angels demand it."

I remembered the glowing angel. Did his sort visit a place like this or only leafy graves in Connecticut? I supposed they must – children were children the world over.

Our stay came to an end. We were taking one last stroll around the garden, when Janet suddenly stopped in front of a large beech. Hanging from a lower branch was an ancient home-made swing – just ropes knotted through a wooden plank. She didn't speak for a little while, then:

"It's just come to me how Charlotte Beauvais died. She fell off that swing and struck her head. We must only have been four or five years old. I wonder why father never removed it."

My good mood plummeted. Charlie… Missing him still tore me in two. I thought of him less often, but the pain never went away.

"Did Charlie ever visit?" I gasped

"Naturally not - it was years before he was born."

"Before you ask, no I don't think visiting his grave in Caen would be a good idea. It would make you relive the whole tragedy."

I was disappointed but she was right.

When we got back to the car, I saw her turn in a full circle, committing the place to memory one last time. She was moist-eyed but resigned and smiled at me and shrugged.

"I'm pleased I came, even though it breaks my heart to leave it for the last time."

We kissed the girls and hugged Marianna. Jonathan kissed our hands, then we got in the car, more determinedly American than when we came.

Chapter Thirty-three

Last Goodbye to a Beloved Friend

I stopped at Annandale, my third home, for a couple of days before going back to Windham.

Janet and I, late the evening before I left, moved Trina's tiny casket. Between us we managed to lever the stone slab open with the help of a crowbar she had sneaked from the garage.

We placed Katrina alongside Isobel's urn. Janet gently lay a small bunch of the last rosebuds of summer between them. We replaced the stone and slid the altar back. Trina's name would remain on the stone outside, which I kissed after we'd remade the grave and covered it with leaves. Before we set off for home, we both leaned against the chapel wall to regain our strength. And to say a small private prayer for our baby girls.

When a faint but distinct glow trailed between the trees, we smiled at each other, knowing it'd been the right thing to do.

Duncan walked over to say goodbye. He shook me by the hand. Bill hugged me. Janet did too but with rather more enthusiasm than usual it appeared to me. Perhaps it was in thanks for our shared secrets.

It was a quiet journey back. I stopped off at a roadhouse near Pittsburg, grabbed something to eat and slept for a few hours.

The wind off the lake was sharp when I arrived home, so I had the girls light the sitting room fire and picked up the mail from the brass charger in the hall.

On the top was a brown envelope stamped Western Union. It was a telegram from Bill. Janet's heart had failed, and she had died in the conservatory two hours after I'd left.

I felt absolutely nothing. After all the trauma around Charlie and Trina's deaths, not to mention the murder of my own husband, when my dearest friend left, I was numb.

I rang Bill and asked what he wanted me to do. Despite their bored marriage, now that she'd gone, he seemed totally adrift.

Janet and Alec had both left him, and Oliver had ceased to exist. There was only me and Duncan. She had already been moved to a Chapel of Rest and they were in the process of working with the funeral director on the details. By the time I got there, there would be nothing for me to do. Could I send flowers and perhaps visit in a few weeks when calm had returned?

His only immediate request was that I let Oliver know. Perhaps he felt now Janet was gone he would be able to rebuild bridges.

Perhaps it was so Janet could haunt their grandson for the rest of his days. She'd like that.

Darn it! I'd have to break my own rules. But it was the only thing requested of me so I couldn't say no.

I flew to Los Angeles, and rather than travelling to San Clemente, booked into the International Hotel at the airport.

First job, I contacted a florist in Danbury and had an enormous bouquet of roses sent like those on my trellis at Windham, intertwined with white orchids. I wanted to let her know how loved she'd been. It was strange in retrospect, I never doubted she was still with me – as if she was in the next room. Perhaps that's why I hadn't grieved like I had with the others.

To find Oliver, I tried the White Pages first. There were so many Maxwells, it seemed the whole of the Scottish border had decamped to Los Angeles.

I couldn't go to the police for obvious reasons, so eventually I resorted to using a P.I. It took him precisely twenty-four hours. When I gave him all the information I could, he decided to trace Rachel rather than Oliver and found her at an address in Bel Air. Oh well, I'd have 'to beard the lion in his den'.

Early the following morning I drove there. He'd done pretty well with the money I'd given him. His mansion looked like something out of 'Gone with the Wind', with gardens which made Windham's look like a postage stamp. They were beautiful but for the twee little pagoda which took up the whole of one corner and had a moat round it.

I'd been psyching myself up all the way there, but as luck would have it just as I turned the car around to park, a dark blue European soft top roared out of the drive so fast it'd to swerve to avoid a couple of motors half-parked on the sidewalk. I took it that was the joker I'd given birth to.

A figure came hurtling down the asphalt after it, somewhat pointlessly as she was on foot and the car had disappeared at breakneck speed.

I'd only seen her on a couple of occasions but recognized Rachel instantly – mostly because you'd to concentrate hard to separate her from her surroundings. She just seemed to fade in.

She'd light brown hair and a pale complexion, at present a bit blotchy. I couldn't believe it when she reached the end of the drive gasping for breath and placed the back of her hand to her forehead for all the world like some heroine in a black and white melodrama.

"Oliver…., my darling…," her voice got progressively more strident. "Oh, do come home, Oliver."

Then she saw me and stopped dead. You could have cut the silence with a knife.

"Oh!," she said – or more precisely – "Ew!," her voice switching effortlessly from L.A. to Hyannis.

Oh well, in for a penny… I got out of the car and walked towards her. She looked as if she might bolt but after a quick assessment, decided I might possibly be the faster, so she stood stiff as a poker at the end of her own drive and waited for me to speak.

"Good morning. Rachel Litton-Thomas or is it Maxwell?" She straightened her shoulders, and in a stronger voice said:

"Mrs. Maxwell. A pleasure – what a surprise." *Yes, I'll bet.* "You just missed Oliver. He's gone to work." Then a deep breath and concentrated effort later:

"Won't you come in and take tea? I have some petit fours."

Janet would have been legless with laughter, but I kept a straight face and followed her the half mile to the front door. Neither of us spoke.

After she'd called her kitchen maid with instructions to make the tea, she extended a blue-veined hand. She had lovely hands, I noticed – long, tapering fingers with well-manicured nails. Despite circumstances, her handshake was firm. I liked that.

We 'took tea' from faux Minton chinaware, she with her pinkie finger in the air. All the time, she was glancing out of the window, nervously checking Oliver didn't return.

"Do relax, dear," I said, exasperated. "By the speed he left, he's probably in San Francisco by now. He won't be back for a while."

She did unwind a little and sipped her tea.

"I'll get straight to the point," I said. "Oliver's grandmother has died. His grandfather lives in Connecticut. He didn't think it appropriate the news be passed on over the phone. So here I am, much against my will, and knowing Oliver won't give a shit."

She grimaced at my language.

"Oh, goddam!," I said scrabbling about in my purse for a tissue. I noticed with some satisfaction she'd gone from pale to translucent. But that wasn't fair. She might be married to Oliver, but he was more my fault than hers.

She stood to replenish my cup, her self-control exemplary – I'd have thrown me out by now.

It was then I saw she was pregnant. If she hadn't been so frail, I probably wouldn't have noticed. I didn't know what to ask first – when did they get married or when was the baby due or even, was the one connected to the other. Or were they married at all?

She must have noticed both my glance and my hesitation.

"We got married at City Hall a month ago."

'City Hall? Cheapskate!'

"We had planned to get married in any case," she was quick to add.

Yes, I thought but the difference was a summer dress in an office or a flower-bedecked Cathedral in a Helen Rose gown. There was a deal of sympathy in my smile, and I felt her unfreeze slightly.

"The baby is due in the Spring. If it's a boy, he's to be called Matthew after my Fairbrother grandfather, and if it's a girl she'll be Dorcas or Deborah – perhaps Delilah. But Oliver doesn't think that goes with Maxwell so maybe one of the other two. We haven't decided."

Her voice, initially full of brightness, trailed off. It wasn't difficult to see she was unhappy, but then she put her foot in it bigtime.

"Perhaps we should call her Grace. Oliver might like her to be named for his mother."

"Don't hold your breath," I said wryly.

Bill might not have thought it suitable to pass on the news by phone, so I wrote Oliver a note instead. It read:

"I've been tasked with letting you know your grandmother had a heart attack and died at Annandale last Sunday evening.

The funeral is Saturday at two-thirty in the afternoon. Grandpa has been kind enough to request your presence at the family chapel on the Annandale estate. If you can't

~~go (or don't want to)~~ *feel unable to attend, I know he would be touched by a bunch of flowers.*

I won't be there.

Grace

I left my first thoughts scored through so he could see what I really believed, and I couldn't bring myself to write 'Mom' or even 'Mother'. The last was by way of encouragement for him to go.

"Please forgive me, Mrs. Maxwell, but I have to go finish the months business accounts. Oliver gets annoyed if they're not ready on time."

"Accounts?"

"Yes, I really love numbers so it's no hardship and it does help him out – and saves him some money."

She looked around surreptitiously, as if about to share a confidence perhaps she shouldn't.

"We live in this big house but we're not as well off as you might suppose. He relies on me to squeeze every penny out of the business. I don't think he would mind *you* knowing though," she whispered.

I swallowed the remains of my tea, picked up my purse and hightailed it out of there before they could hear me swearing in Halifax.

Goddam son-of-a-bitch! He could buy the Dodgers twice over and he had his pregnant wife screwing every penny she could out of the IRS.

I'd fulfilled my obligations. I went home.

Chapter Thirty-four
The Kailua Kid

I did go back to Annandale not long after Christmas. I felt I needed to visit Janet's grave. Perhaps the angel would comfort her too. He would, I knew it.

After, I pushed back the altar in the chapel, kissed our little girls goodnight, and said a silent prayer for Charlie.

It seemed much that was most dear to me lay in those few square yards of land.

Bill was staying with Duncan. He'd left a skeleton staff at Annandale who gave me directions. I'd never visited Duncan's remote farm before. It was an easier walk than car ride, so I took off over the fields as directed.

Bill had never been a demonstrative man and Janet definitely wore the pants, but I was unprepared for what I found. He was clearly distraught.

Duncan got out the Glenfiddich, but it looked as if Bill'd sunk half a bottle already. Not exactly fit for visitors. Duncan looked at me apologetically. Why he felt he had to apologize I couldn't say, but it was clear visitors were not wanted at that moment.

After a somewhat slurred and absurd attempt at conversation, I took Duncan to one side. I wrote down my numbers at Windham and Ginsling and asked if he would call me when Bill had had time to recover.

He and Bill had taken Oliver to their hearts, and he had screwed them time and time again. Duncan asked if I'd been able to get a message through to him about the funeral. I lied through my teeth and said I hadn't. Better the blame fell on me than they were disappointed again.

Duncan offered to run me back to Annandale, but I opted to return as I'd come, pick up my hire car and head out to the airport. I would be exhausted by the time I got home to Illinois, but I didn't feel like hanging around in a New York hotel. I took the first flight I could get.

Bill wasn't the only one knocked for a loop by Janet's death. My best friend and mentor was gone. Once the numbness had worn off and the crippling pain of her passing had set in, I locked myself away at Windham, feeling absolutely and completely alone, deserted. I walked my gardens and gazed moodily out across the lake, drinking more than was good for me and smoking cigarette after cigarette.

By April, I'd finally come to the conclusion I'd have to think of something to do soon. I was boring myself to death and the servants were getting lax.

I gave them all a kick in the ass again and began a Spring clean to restore order . I tied my hair up in a scarf, donned overalls and stripped every bit of linen from every single room. Two of the parlor maids were tasked with washing it, and it hung on a line stretched across the garden like flags on a naval schooner.

The phone rang as I was stripping the hall of rugs. Both hands occupied, I wedged the receiver in the crook of my neck and yelled:

"Yes?"

"It's Geoff Litton-Thomas, Mrs. Maxwell."

I dropped the rugs in a heap on the floor.

"The other two didn't seem inclined to call, but I thought it important you know you are a grandmother. A little boy, Matthew, six pounds twelve ounces. Mother and son are doing well – now. It was touch and go with Rachel for a while but she's okay."

My heart melted. The sins of the father should not be visited on an innocent child.

"Likewise, congratulations. What happened to Rachel?"

"As you know she is small, and the strain of carrying the baby caused a heart murmur. The doctors don't think it serious, and it should resolve itself over time."

"I do hope she will be well soon. Which hospital is she in? I'll send some flowers. I don't know if you know, but my son and I are estranged and likely to remain that way. A visit would not be welcome."

"They've moved Rachel and the baby to the UCLA Centre for a few days observation, so I'm sure she'd appreciate the flowers."

Well, flowers for a funeral and flowers for a birth all within six months.

I hadn't heard from Duncan, so once I'd scrubbed the house clean, I called him. Bill had ricocheted the other way apparently and was currently holidaying in Hawaii. Duncan was as mystified as I. Oh well, clearly he was all right – for the present at least.

I'd had a rough winter, so I packed and left for San Clemente, on a beautiful day in May.

Janet was gone and Evie was back in Nevada. One is a lonely number when it comes to dining out, but I didn't really care except that I was so bored. By the end of two weeks, I'd walked every inch of the town, so I jumped in my car and drove through heaven-scented orange and lemon groves in full flower.

I ended up in the very same little town where a chance meeting led me to acquire the most loyal member of my staff. God knows why little Tina Lopez had chosen to stick by me. It wasn't as if I was nice to her. Through the worst of my losses, tantrums, depressions and frustrations she'd been there.

On the way back, I picked up some tomatoes and peppers from the grocery store, steak and fries from a take-out and treated Tina and her co-workers to lunch in the garden. As I watched them laughing together on the lawn, it hit me forcefully that I was no longer a spring chicken and my aches and pains had nothing to do with sitting in a draught. How old was I? Forty something? Oh, my Lord....

It was decades since I'd first set foot on American soil! During that time, I'd been companion to a gangster's moll who showered me with untold riches for reasons best known to herself, become soul mates with a Scottish aristocrat, met the love of my life and given birth to Beelzebub. God, that was depressing.

I poured myself a large gin and went to sit on a garden seat by a lilac-blue rhododendron. Blue like my mood. I sighed and threw the rest of the alcohol into the road.

So, what *was* I good at? Nothing really. I was pretty much self-educated, and I had money to burn. Not a lot of scope there.

I used to enjoy reading Shakespeare in Marcia's library. *MARCIA'S LIBRARY!* All my books were still at Annandale! That would give me something constructive to do. I'd made a purpose-built room for them at Ginsling. I'd totally forgotten.

I went to Annandale and got the sad bit of my journey over with first – visiting Janet, who I chatted to for a while, saying my customary prayer for the babies, and sending loving thoughts to Charlie. I should time my calls for such days. It was less painful when birds sang joyfully amongst the leaves.

I got the shock of my life when I went to pick up the books.

Bill was sitting out front in a Hawaiian shirt with parrots on it and a pair of shorts. He must have lost at least forty pounds and had had his hair styled to hide his encroaching baldness. He was humming tunelessly to himself as he cleaned an elderly-looking rifle, dismantling it.

I came close to losing my lunch. I found myself reliving that horrific day in the garden cabin.

Bill saw me, put down his oily rag and sauntered over. The humming turned into whistling. I wasn't sure what was going on here. I stood still until the situation became clearer.

"Gracie – my little Gracie!," and he picked me up under the armpits and swung me round as if I was still in grade school. Little Gracie – hadn't I just figured I was in my forties? Still when you were in your seventies, perhaps forties *was* 'little', so I decided to cut him some slack.

"Hello, Bill – well look at you! Aren't you just a dandy!"

He put me down and turned three-sixty degrees so I could take a good look.

"Hired one of those personal stylists like they do in Hollywood. Good, eh?"

"Books still where I left them, Bill?"

There didn't seem to be anything else to say.

"Sure are."

Fortunately, at that moment the haulage truck arrived, and I showed them to the bedroom where my books were stored, passing a whistling Bill on the way. He'd gone back to his gun cleaning.

An hour later I watched the truck trundle down the drive, patted Bill on the cheek and smiled tersely.

"Well, guess I'll see you around," said Bill, suddenly looking a little less confident.

"Possibly. Next time I come to visit Janet," I said, putting emphasis on her name. I paused for a moment to reconsider. "Yes, perhaps."

I got in my hire car, drove back to the airport and flew back to LA. then I travelled to San Clemente to await my books.

Halfway through the flight I burst out laughing so hard the stewardess had to bring me some water. The only upside of this would have been the look on Oliver's face, as he introduced his bride and in-laws to his seventy-six-year-old grandpapa wearing a Hawaiian shirt and shorts.

Which reminded me…. I'd forgotten to tell Bill he was a great grandpa.

Chapter Thirty-five

Matt, the Minx and 'Gwanny Gwace'

I was in the throes of sorting out the books and fitting them on their shelves when Tina bustled in to tell me there was a young lady at the door asking for me.

Rachel was in the process of unhooking the cutest little baby I'd ever seen from his car seat. I'm mostly not impressed by the little darlings and find them smelly, wet and unhygienic. I certainly wasn't inclined to nurse them on my knee, but she handed Matthew over to me as she collected his bag and belongings, and I instantly lost my heart. He was a delight.

Huge sapphire-blue eyes smiled up at me through long golden lashes. He reached up and patted me on the cheek as if we were old friends. This was a keeper. Rachel could go back to Oliver now.

She smiled at me in her nervous way and shook my hand. Even I wasn't that formal. I hugged her…. briefly. Fortunately, the baby precluded anything more.

"Oliver wouldn't come so I thought I'd bring Matthew to meet you."

She looked around as if my son might leap out from behind the nearest rhododendron, bit like she had at Bel Air.

"He doesn't know I'm here. I don't know why he won't come," she ended wistfully.

"He won't come because I won't allow it. There are reasons, but they're between Oliver and me. If you want to know, you'll have to ask him."

I was a little brusquer than perhaps I'd intended but speaking of our situation always made me feel sick. I'd have loved to be a fly on the wall when Oliver told his patrician wife he'd broken his father's skull with a gun stock, but hell would freeze over before that happened.

I wasn't going to give Matthew back just yet. His mother fluttered with anxiety as I led her to the terrace.

"Are you breast-feeding…," I automatically looked down at her flat chest, then "or would you like me to warm a bottle for you?"

His little face puckered into a grimace closely followed by a loud fart and a horrendous smell. I handed him back. Rachel laid out a plastic sheet on my dining table, wiped his disgusting bottom and poked about in her bag for a clean diaper. Perhaps it was at this point Oliver and I had lost touch.

Rachel pointed at the bag, and I found the bottle filled with formula. I was just about to call Tina to warm it, then decided I'd rather take it to the kitchen myself. I needed the air.

When I returned, she handed him back to me, now disinfected and smelling sweetly of baby powder. Matt – for clearly he was never going to be a Matthew - looked up at me and grinned broadly as if somehow he'd scored a point.

I stuck the teat between his lips, and he looked me directly in the eye and actually giggled. When he started to bloat, I put him over my shoulder to rub his back and he promptly vomited. I'd like to bet he was still grinning as he did it.

I'd a couple more clandestine visits from Rachel after that, then they abruptly stopped so I assumed Oliver had intervened. I was surprised how much I missed Matt. Couldn't say the same for his mother. She drank tea with her pinkie raised and spoke through her nose like the Kennedys.

I busied myself with organizing my library, thinking I might hire a tutor. Literature? Or a language – Spanish might be good in Southern California. I might then understand what Tina was babbling on about when I'd clearly upset her.

Two years after Matt, another grandchild arrived. A little girl - Deborah Janet. If that was meant to soften up Oliver's grandfather, he was barking up the wrong tree. I doubted the Kailua Kid even remembered his existence. Last I'd heard from Duncan, Bill had acquired a lady friend.

I was absolutely amazed when Oliver himself brought the baby to see me when she was about six months old. He must have known he was taking a chance after the deal we'd made. He told me Rachel was back in hospital. She'd had a more severe recurrence of her heart problem during her labor and had to return to hospital from time to time. I wondered who was doing his accounts.

Deborah had the same bright blue eyes as Matt, who was grimly concentrating on putting one foot in front of the other without falling over. It was easy to see Oliver was losing patience.

I picked Matt up out of the way, and he promptly poked me in the eye, grabbed my face between his hands and held it fast. He didn't want me looking at the usurper.

My initial observation of Deborah suggested she cried if someone wasn't holding her. She loved attention. Then I noticed she smelled sweeter than Matt even with a full diaper.

I didn't know how they came to have such beautiful children – Oliver was okay I guess but Rachel was no oil painting. Matt's hair had darkened as he'd grown but Deborah's was pure white. She was going to be a beauty.

"This is wrong, Oliver. You absolutely can't come here. I don't want to see you and you took the money to stay away. What the hell are you doing here? Do you *want* me to call the cops?"

"No – don't be stupid, of course I don't"

I could feel my temperature rising. If he spoke to me like that again, kids or no kids, he'd be getting the same treatment he doled out to his dad. He clearly noticed the smoke coming out of my ears because he went on in a more conciliatory manner:

"Look… I don't want us to fall out again. Wouldn't you like to see your grandchildren from time to time?"

Matt grabbed my head again and pulled his hands back and forth to make me nod. Then he whispered in my ear:

"Please Gwanny Gwace. Please…."

I looked at him fiercely, but his eyes were fixed on mine, and he refused to look away.

"Well, looks like that's your answer."

My face was grim.

Deborah who'd been asleep in Oliver's arms, had woken and begun to whitter, which quickly turned into a full-throttled yell. He jigged her up and down, smiling into her face until she shut up. Easy to see the favoritism had begun.

Matt was starting to get heavy, so I sat down with him on my knee. Oliver remained standing.

"Well?" he said. I looked from him to Matt who turned his head into my shoulder.

"Okay. I don't want to see you, but I'll take the kids out an afternoon each week. It'll give Rachel a break anyway."

She clearly hadn't been included in his calculations, but he quickly understood the lever he'd been given.

"I'm sure she would appreciate that very much. She prefers figures to kids anyway."

He left, rapping Matt sharply on the rear when he wouldn't let go of my neck.

"Tina, pon un poco de café en la biblioteca. Estare ocupado por un par de horas."

My Spanish wasn't brilliant, but it stretched to coffee in the library. I sometimes wondered what I actually had said because Tina occasionally hid an ill-suppressed grin behind her apron. Still, she appreciated I was trying, so reciprocated. She seemed to have a problem with tenses. I wondered if I had too.

I determined to read every book I'd placed on the shelves. But first I took the precious Shakespeare folio to a printers' shop in town and got them the look at the spine. Some of the leaves were loosening.

They reinforced the attachments and gave the leather cover a professional clean as I| requested. But when I asked, they acquiesced through clenched teeth as it would reduce its value. How peculiar – a house price increased when you cleaned it first.

As I was replacing it horizontally on its own shelf, I wondered if I could find another – 'Romeo and Juliet' or 'The Taming of the Shrew' for instance. I contacted a couple of auction houses. They were very dubious and said originals were usually regarded as museum pieces. It didn't stop them asking how much I wanted for mine though.

Chapter Thirty-six

Grace and Connie Connect

My trips out with the kids sometimes extended to as much as two complete days, when I brought them to San Clemente and let them run riot on the beach.

They both loved the sea and once Matt had turned six, he was already an accomplished swimmer. Deborah was happy to splash about in the shallows and at four was still at the sandcastle stage. I bought her little paper flags to poke into the tops of the towers.

Matt took care of her, taking her hand when she fell, fetching her ice cream, drying her tears. She repaid him by kicking sand in his face then laughing when he cried. He never retaliated – sometimes I wished he had. I fumed. She needed a damn good spanking.

But she was nobody's fool, even at that age. Eventually, she coerced Oliver into letting her stay at home with her Mom.

I was only in Rachel's company occasionally when I collected the children, and Oliver I didn't see at all. They both hated being around the kids but had different ways of dealing with it. Rachel would disappear into her office with a mug of coffee and lock the door. For Oliver it was easiest to ignore sunny-natured Matt and give in to Deborah's every whim. She was a sneaky little madam and an appalling taleteller, but her Dad was well and truly wound around her little finger – or too disinterested to care. They deserved each other.

Matt felt unloved, ignored and miserable. He loved me fiercely which his stupid parents could never understand.

Then overnight it seemed, everything changed.

It began with Rachel leaving. She packed up lock stock and barrel and went back to her parents, leaving the children with Oliver. It didn't matter how Deborah screamed and stamped her foot she never came back. Oliver heaped expensive gifts on his little girl to keep her quiet.

Matt would sit in the garden pagoda, sheltered by the wisteria and shake with fright. He was only seven. He didn't even know how to call me. But the shock made him learn.

I don't know why Rachel left – I never asked. Frankly, I never much cared.

The next I heard – maybe six months later – Oliver had another woman. The only thing I knew about her was her name, and I drew the conclusion she couldn't have been right in her head. Or she was desperate.

By this time, I was getting chapter and verse from Matt, who had made it his business to learn how to use a telephone.

She was called Connie and – apparently – she was very pretty. She had two sons who seemed to come and go. He quite liked one of them who was called Jake.

Deborah hated Connie. She'd taken her mom away, she said. I doubted she even cared about Rachel's absence, other than as a way to force her Dad to give her even more of what she wanted. And possibly make Matt's life even more miserable.

After a while, a man had started turning up at the house. He smelled funny and had to lean on things. He shouted a lot and was scary. Daddy got furious when he came. He yelled at Connie although Matt couldn't figure out why. Something to do with a baserd – 'what's one of those, Grannie?'

Then one day Connie went to stay with this strange man. Matt cried on the phone. He wanted me to tell him what to do. I had no idea at all what to say to him.

Matt was desperate for Connie to come back. He said she was kind – she made jam tarts with him and let him lick the spoon, and they had built a library together for his books.

The strange man had turned out to be Connie's husband and he was sick in hospital. Dad called it rehab, but Connie explained to Matt that that was a place for people to get well again, so really it was a kind of hospital. She had gone to help her husband until he felt better. Matt couldn't think why Dad was upset about that. It seemed a kind thing to do.

Poor Oliver. His life had become so complicated. How sad.

When Connie left, Oliver was morose, Deborah cock-a-hoop and Matt walked six miles to her home to find her and beg her to come back.

A short time later, he rang to tell me she had come home. He was laughing and crying by turns with relief. Oh, that poor little wretch. If only I could take him away with me. It wasn't worth even asking - Matt would suffer if I did.

Amazingly, the next phone call was from Oliver. He wanted to bring this Connie and her two sons to meet me. Why in God's name would he do that? And Matt and Deborah he said as an afterthought.

I liked Connie on sight, although doubted her sanity. She was proud and outspoken but a lady to the core. She drank coffee with her finger in, so Janet would have approved.

It didn't take Oliver long to get to the point. Rachel had walked out so he was ditching her for this woman.

Of course, with Connie there he didn't quite put it like that, but that was the way it was. Seemed to me Rachel had already done the ditching. Still, one less misfit to contend with couldn't be bad. Unless I was misjudging Connie which I felt I wasn't.

I carted her off to my library out of the way. She was very impressed by my Shakespeare folio, and nearly fainted when I banged it down on the library table for her to look at. She was clearly educated enough to realize its worth.

I was relieved that at last poor Matt had the break he deserved. It was clear she had taken him to her heart.

I got the impression she was as lonely as he was. There was a shattering story behind her eyes – I saw it clearly in her expression and the way she would avoid looking at me when discussing anything she found difficult. She also had a habit of tugging at her little finger. Yes, she was good friend material and clearly desperately in need of someone herself. What in God's name was she doing with Oliver?

For some reason she felt she owed me an explanation.

"Deborah doesn't like me – blames me for her mother leaving, I think. You must believe me Mrs. Maxwell...."

"Grace..." I said through gritted teeth.

".... Grace, I had nothing to do with their separation. I came along much later."

"No matter. You and Rachel will have behaved impeccably. It's the other one who bothers me."

On the second day of their stay, we took the kids down to the beach, then to eat on the pier.

Later of course, Deborah fucked everything up. She was enough to make a saint swear. She'd shoved Connie's little one down a flight of marble stairs and broken his ankle.

Afterwards, the little bitch was twiddling her curls round her finger, sitting on daddy's knee and playing the innocent. She grinned – I smiled nastily back. I was about to exact my revenge. She wasn't used to retaliation, so she batted her eyelids at Oliver and buried her face in his chest.

We got Connie's kid patched up at the hospital, then I told Oliver I was going home in the morning and taking Deborah with me for some quality time together. I smiled lovingly at his daughter. For once, she didn't smile back.

Lots of things happened simultaneously then. Oliver, for once, was speechless. Connie moved back into the shadows trying to maintain a straight face, and Deborah jumped off her dad's knee and screamed. Underneath it all I had the distinct impression 'daddy' was relieved. He didn't say anything.

Matt, poor thing, was sobbing, torn between fear at what he knew his sister had coming and concern for his friend.

238

He was sitting on the stairs. Connie sat next to him and dried his tears. He put both arms round her and buried his head at her breast. They were a comfort to each other.

I couldn't believe the expression on Oliver's face. He was actually jealous of his own infant son. I couldn't begin to imagine how he felt about Connie's husband. It must be eating him alive, poor thing.

Of course, Deborah's visit to Windham was every bit as devastating as she'd imagined. I had her hang up her own clothes and make her own bed. When she refused, she ended up having to make mine as well.

She retaliated by refusing to wash so she went dirty – for three whole days, during which time she was allowed no clean clothes. She felt less than a 'little princess' once the staff started avoiding her.

Then all she wanted to eat was tacos and she refused anything else. Such was her resolve it was a whole day before she tucked into chicken casserole and dumplings, which she shoveled down in desperation.

By day four she was sitting on a chair in the kitchen, helping a maid she'd taken a shine to to shell peas. She appeared to be eating more than went in the pot but at least she was doing something useful

.

On day five I allowed her a call to her Dad and went and stood behind the door, listening. She never stopped to draw breath, telling him how she'd been locked in the cellar and fed bread and water or some such nonsense. She was so over the top, even he didn't believe her. That earned her an extra day in my clutches as I made sure she knew.

On day six, I took her back to LA. At the airport, Connie picked her up, kissed me affectionately in full view of the little madam and smiled at Deborah's frustration. I had no doubt at all she would be back to her usual self within a couple of days, but she had provided me with almost a week's entertainment, so I couldn't complain.

"…and if you have any more problems," I said loudly, "you can always send her back."

I was very gratified to see my granddaughter blanche.

Chapter Thirty-seven

The House-guest

I was at Windham before my next encounter with my son. And a very fortuitous one it turned out to be. None of us realized at the time how completely our lives would be shattered by future events. Nothing for any of us would ever be the same again.

Oliver arrived unbidden on my doorstep. He looked like shit – clothes rumpled, hair uncombed and white as a sheet.

"What the hell happened to you? And what are you doing here – *again*?," I asked, less than sympathetic, "Don't just stand there – come in before your late father's ghost makes his nightly appearance."

He brushed past me and sat on a hall chair.

"Need a drink?," I asked laconically.

"Large….and bring the bottle. We're both going to need it."

I couldn't imagine anything which would upset us both at the same time, so I was intrigued.

"You'd better come into the sitting room, then."

We relocated and I brought us both a large brandy from the sideboard. He was shaking like a leaf and gulped down half the glass in one.

"It's Connie…."

"Yes, I liked her – and her kids," a poke at the lovely Deborah. "She's welcome at San Clemente……"

"…...You might change your mind after what I'm about to tell you," he broke in. "She's pregnant."

"Congratulations."

"I had a vasectomy after Deborah was born – not mine.

Its Gil's."

"Oh dear, that is unfortunate. What are you going to do?"

"Do you think I should throw her out? I love her but this is the ultimate betrayal!"

"It's not for me to say what you should do. It's your mess to sort out - not mine."

He walked to the window and stared out at the tranquil lake.

"The kid will have to go. How could I explain it to Deborah and Matt? She doesn't want it brought up by that son-of-a-bitch – drunken, drug-addled bastard. She doesn't even want him to know about the birth, in case he does the same again as he did to her and her other two."

"Seems you have a real problem this time. Any further thought other than getting rid of the baby?"

I offered him a bit of rope to hang himself.

"No way would she have an abortion. We've been down that road.."

Well, the complete bastard. If someone had suggested that when I was carrying Trina, I'd have been devastated. In fact, my heart bled for Connie.

This was a complete replay of part of my life, and Charlie came to mind so strongly that for the very first time I saw him. Behind his shoulder was another face I almost didn't recognize without its glow, but the kind, supportive expression was the same. In the blink of an eye, both visions had vanished.

"You'd better fetch Connie here. If you won't sort it, I'll have to. You weren't supposed to come back once I'd made you a millionaire. I should tell you to go to hell.

"Leave. You're not staying here. I'm doing this for Connie."

He must have gone straight home, sent the kids to Rachel's and dragged Connie straight here, because they were back in three days.

He'd composed himself, but Connie looked as if she'd been pulled through a hedge.

"Go to hell, Oliver." I ordered.

The self-satisfied grin he gave me as he left to return home, confirmed my next course of action. I poured Connie some soda water.

"I want the whole story – start to finish. Nothing left out because you think you might offend me. Nothing left out because you are ashamed. I want the lot, beginning to end. Stop crying. It's not productive."

I handed her a box of tissues. One of the girls came in to enquire about refreshments.

"OUT!," I yelled at the poor girl.

"The baby is due in January. If it's not Oliver's it has to be Gil's. There's no other alternative, but I would have thought that a slim chance........."

She'd told Gil. He was distraught at her decision to keep him away from his child. What the hell could possibly justify their separation? Not Oliver, that was for sure.

The afternoon turned into evening before she was done. One last morning of unrestrained ecstasy had produced a lovechild in the true sense of the word. My own eyes filled with tears for what might have been for us both.

Circumstance had made me a bitter woman. With her soul in her eyes, the poor girl said:

"I don't know what else to say. My mother won't have me, and Oliver says he can't. I don't know what to do." She had badly misconstrued my own earlier tears.

I called Oliver and told him to pack Connie's belongings and send them to Windham. He deserved no explanation, and he got none. He didn't seem to care. Why should he when the situation had been offloaded onto me?

He sent Connie's things freight, and only called a couple of times during the months she was at Windham. He made no appearance. God only knows what was happening to my Matt. He always took the brunt of Oliver's moods, and this time it would be terrible.

Poor Connie didn't leave her room for two days. Shame as much as tiredness I guessed. I had her meals sent up, but she hardly touched them. Then on the third morning, she ate all her breakfast and came downstairs to face me. I hugged her for a good five minutes, as much for my sake as hers.

"You are being more a mother to me than my own," she said gravely. "I will never be able to repay you, but I want you to know I am grateful from the bottom of my heart."

"Yes, well. Let's not make a meal of it. Come and sit in here. You've said your piece. Now it's my turn."

Her whole demeanor turned to one of trepidation.

"Oh, not like that. Just something I'd like you to do in return."

"Anything…"

"I want you to ask no questions now – what you don't know you can't accidentally pass on. I want you to have the baby born and registered in Los Angeles. Your mother'll just have to deal with it."

Connie hid a smile – the first in a long time, I suspected.

"Then the child must be adopted privately since a formal adoption would throw up a paper-trail for Gil to follow," I warned.

I remembered what Janet had told me when I'd considered having Trina adopted – it would tear the heart out of her to let her baby go.

Then all hell was let loose. Thoughtlessly, I was so taken up with Connie and the baby, I'd forgotten this was a triangle.

Connie and Matthew had been visiting Windham. Connie had just tucked him in bed when the phone rang - it was Gil. He'd checked in with Oliver as a last resort, and the son-of-a-bitch had given him my number. Unbelievable!

Connie could clearly tell Gill'd been taking something. I saw her stiffen. She spoke in a whisper for a few minutes, replaced the receiver and came and sat down next to me, then turned her head and sobbed into my shoulder. I pushed her away and told her to explain.

His speech was slurred, she said, and he was barely coherent. Apparently, his mother had been trying to locate her and was worried to death. No one had been able to find her. Gil was getting ready for a concert and told his mother he'd call back but didn't until the following afternoon.

Then Connie hit him with both barrels – she told him about her pregnancy, told him it was his, then told him to go to hell. I can only assume it was because he'd fallen off the wagon again. Then she put the phone down. And that was the end of that – except although she did her best to hide it, I saw her heart had shattered.

Lovers' tiffs are never without emotion but this was different. For Connie it was cataclysmic.

Chapter Thirty-eight

Connie learns of the Pay-off

In desperation, I wracked my brain for some – any - kind of immediate solution. I eventually thought of something I hoped would be a comfort to her although, like all 'best laid plans' it could go disastrously wrong.

I'd take her to Annandale and show her giving up her baby wasn't the end of the world – at least there was a real chance of them reuniting in the future. There was an infinitely worse scenario.

"Come along and I'll show you a part of my life even Oliver doesn't know about. You will please promise you will keep this between us. The fewer people who know about my past the better. Parts of it are not all sweetness and light."

Momentarily, she forgot her own problems and looked at me curiously.

"I'm going to take you to meet someone. Well, four someones actually. Hold onto your hat for a surprise. I'll begin to cue you in on the flight. By way of preparation, I'll tell you I was not born American, I'm originally English."

By the time we got to New York, I'd told her about Ellis Island and Addie, Marcia and my inheritance, Alec, Janet and Bill. I saved Charlie and my war-time catastrophe including Trina for later.

I intended telling her the whole shebang, no matter the cost to me, but all at once might not be a good idea. However, she deserved this chance to come to terms with her own situation.

We took a cab from the station to Annandale, and I banged on the door as I did so many years ago, when Janet was unknown, and Alec a callow youth.

Bill answered the door himself, polishing a brass ornament with his ubiquitous oily rag. Damn if he wasn't still wearing a Hawaiian shirt and shorts – not the same ones thankfully. He looked older – no doubt the personal stylist was now history.

"Hi, Bill. We've come to stay for a couple of days. Hope you don't mind," I said, sliding past him into the hall, tugging Connie with me.

"No, 'course not – book room do?,"

"No. It wasn't too clean, as I recall." He turned round and yelled:

"Doraaa! Get the front double cleaned out. Gracie brought a friend."

That poor woman – she'd stuck with the Maxwells through thick and thin – mostly thin since Janet died, I guessed. She dashed from the direction of the kitchen, pinnie askew and a smudge on her cheek which looked like oil. Perhaps Bill'd been rubbing her down with his oily cloth too. I smiled to myself at the thought.

Dora dropped a curtsey, grinning from ear to ear. Her black hair had turned white, but her cheeks still retained their youthful flush.

"Glad to see you Miss Grace, Ma'am. Yes, indeed."

Gee her life must have ground to a halt for such enthusiasm.

"I'll fix the room right away, then I'll make some tea. Will you take it in the conservatory?"

Her face fell.

"Mrs. Maxwell would be so cross with me, Ma'am. I have no jam or scones, I'm sorry."

"Oh, Dora, you are such a treasure. Mrs. Maxwell would be delighted just to see you here."

She smiled again and bustled off to get her broom and duster.

"Come on," I said to Connie. "More explanations over tea."

I kissed Bill on the cheek in passing and went to the conservatory. Damn, he'd got rid of some of the planters and installed a jukebox with flashing lights. I unplugged it.

Connie was clearly overwhelmed by this other life of mine. As I intended, along with the rest of the world, she'd seen me as a bitter old harridan who scared the shit out of everyone. People tend not to ask questions of folks like that, and to say my past was checkered was an understatement.

Those who knew most and could be the source of gossip, were Bill who wasn't interested, and Oliver who wouldn't dare. The only person who knew all my secrets, had taken them with her to the grave.

Dora returned with a clean tablecloth and spread it with Janet's Minton tea set. I missed her so much in that moment I cried.

After Dora had fetched the tea and some cheese sandwiches fit for a railways station buffet, I asked her to see we weren't disturbed 'even by Mr. Maxwell'. She dipped again and disappeared, still smiling.

I returned my attention to Connie who'd already picked up on the name Maxwell.

"Bill is Oliver's grandfather so my father-in-law. He's a retired psychiatrist – seems he's gone the way of some of his clients," I said, exasperated. "His wife Janet – my mother-in-law - was the best friend I ever had. She was the kindest, funniest most wonderful person. She had to be."

Almighty shock coming up.

"Did you know Oliver was responsible for his father's death? I paid him off with a million bucks not to come anywhere near me ever again."

I put my hand out to catch her cup, but she'd gone the other way and looked as if she'd been hit with rigor mortis. Her knuckles were white, her face blank and I doubt you could have prized the cup out of her hand with a crowbar.

"It's my fault I haven't enforced that stipulation. Matthew is the apple of my eye. I couldn't forgo seeing him even if that meant I'd to deal with his father again," I forged on.

"He did WHAT!," I gathered we were no longer discussing Matt.

This was the worst news I'd to give her, I hoped.

"At Windham. But not in the house," I added hastily.

I described the circumstances.

She looked on the point of passing out, so I helped her into the sitting room, which hadn't been dusted since Janet died by the look of it, until she regained some of her color. In retrospect, I suppose I could have been more subtle, but I imagined it was a bit like pulling off a sticking plaster – best done quickly.

The room Dora had cleaned was perfect. It had single beds and its own bathroom. I felt happier keeping an eye on Connie. But as it turned out, it wouldn't have mattered anyway since I went out like a light and dreamed of my babies and their protector.

The following day we drove to Danbury, and I showed her my jewels in the bank vaults. She looked at me with her mouth open. I'd told her about Marcia's gangster's moll status, but she hadn't understood the implications of my inheritance. She did now.

I showed her round the town Oliver had known from childhood.

We had a quick peek at Danbury House, which looked dilapidated and had a realtors notice at a precarious angle near the gate.

Lunch was at Alec's favorite little Italian restaurant, surprisingly still there, and with what appeared to be the same menu.

With a great deal of trepidation, I took her to spend some of the afternoon at the Maxwell chapel.

Now that Janet was no longer there, the graves were choked with autumn leaves, which had blown into the chapel, door ajar, and skittered across the blue and white mosaic floor tiles.

I excused myself and stood by my friend's grave for a few minutes. I missed her so much and hoped, wherever she was, she could still understand. I ran my hand lovingly over the top of the marble stone. As I'd expected, the glowing shadow passed between the trees, and I felt comforted. Connie didn't see.

I brushed away the leaves with my hands from the tiny burial and knocked some moss off the headstone so it could be read.

"This is my daughter, Katrina. She died in her cot when she was four months old. She wasn't Alec's child - her father's name was Charles de Riviere Beauvais, a French Count who I loved madly until he was blown to bits by a German shell in Normandy in the war. He was a junior doctor. I was the only survivor from two field medical wards. Everyone else ended up like Charlie.

"I completely collapsed with the trauma of it all. Without Alec and Janet I never could have survived.

"My darling man never knew about his daughter, and she followed him within the year. I have thought about them every single day since. He was the love of my life, and we knew each other so briefly."

"Oh Grace…" Silent tears ran down her cheeks, but there was absolutely nothing she could say.

I got to my feet.

"But she's not buried here anymore," I went on abruptly, "Janet and I dug her up."

I have no idea why Connie giggled. I thought it most inappropriate.

I led her into the chapel and asked her to help me move the altar so she could see the carved slab beneath.

"She's here. Buried with Janet's little girl Isobel who was secretly brought over from Scotland by her mother. Isobel never knew her father either, because he'd left to come here before she was born. She died when she was two years old. We thought they'd appreciate the company although God knows why."

I had resorted to sarcasm to stay strong.

"Alec knew about Trina but married me anyway, before she was born. He was kind and I was so desperately grateful to him, but he was not romance material – not for me, anyway.

"He always knew he'd play second fiddle to Charlie and eventually it inevitably turned our marriage sour. 'course, it didn't help that Janet was more my friend than his mother. She didn't care too much for Alec or Bill, and as she'd found Alec's body, obviously she wasn't too keen on her only grandson either.

"Oliver knows nothing about all this. Neither his aunt Isobel nor his sister Trina, and I'd appreciate it if it stayed that way." Then when she didn't say anything, I added:

"Are you disappointed in me, Connie? I'm not exactly a good example of motherhood. But I wouldn't change one moment of the past and would do it all again in a heartbeat if it would bring him back. You must understand that I love Charlie today as I did all those years ago. And I long for Trina still with a love I never felt for Oliver. I know that makes me a dreadful person, but it's not a thing I have control over."

Walking back to Annandale along the narrow path between the trees, she put her arm round my shoulders and said:

"Thank you, Grace for trusting me."

253

We walked on arm in arm until we reached the house.

We were putting away hats and coats in the closet when Connie said:

"What's the significance of the angel? It's mentioned on both stones."

"Both Janet and I saw him regularly near the children's graves. Our descriptions differed slightly but it was clearly the same.... can you call an angel a person? Anyway, his most arresting feature were his soft eyes filled with such loving kindness. The person – dang.... what are they called? Beings? – I saw looked like a Rembrandt painting but wore black and he glowed. And if you need any more evidence that I've lost my mind, you're deluded too."

I breathed a sigh of relief. My daughter Connie had taken it as I'd hoped and seemed more at peace with herself.

I'd done the best I could. Time to leave Annandale, perhaps for the final time.

There wasn't much conversation on the journey back to Windham. We were both wrapped in our own thoughts. Out of the corner of my eye I saw Connie, gazing out of the plane window, occasionally nodding decisively to herself. She looked calmer, though I knew there were storms still to come.

Chapter Thirty-nine

A Hidden Blessing

The baby came at last. A little girl – a boon to Connie, and in my heart, to me. Only Connie and I knew why this child was so special.

She did all I asked of her, and Anna Robson Maxwell's birth was registered in Los Angeles, then as soon as Connie was able to travel, both of them came to Windham.

Connie stayed with me for three months while she sorted out her affairs.

She had become overly attached to her daughter in a way she never did with her sons. Perhaps it was the upheaval of their life with Gil, and Connie's leaving them with Nancy to follow Oliver, which weakened the link. I couldn't say.

It was true that Connie was devastated when she'd to let the baby go.

We arranged a private adoption which turned out to be easier than I had imagined.

Her adopted parents lived a couple of hundred miles south of Windham in Champaign. Julius Heywood, Anna's adopted father was a lecturer at the University. He and his wife had lost their first child and were told there could be no more.

His wife Catherine suffered severely from depression as a result and Julius had her admitted to a psychiatric clinic, until she was able to cope.

When he heard of Anna through a colleague, I think he would have taken her no matter the circumstances - he had been so afraid his wife would not survive the trauma of her lost child.

Connie had asked that they have her christened and change her name to one of their own choosing. So, Anna Robson Maxwell became Anna Christina Heywood, but was always called Christie, as my Katrina became Trina.

I visited her in Champaign as often as her new parents would allow. They lived in University-provided accommodation, which was a pleasant but unremarkable four bedroomed house overlooking an expanse of green parkland, edged with sugar maple similar to the one I'd planted over Trina's grave.

They'd turned one of the three spare bedrooms into a nursery. It was too pink, fluffy and fairy-bedecked for my taste but I'm sure it was precisely what Cathy had intended.

I turned as I left with one single desperate request of my own, and I have no idea why it was so important to me. As I left, I asked them never to cut her beautiful dark hair. It was as if Trina's angel whispered into my mind how her father would love her long hair as he did before. As a tiny baby of course, she as yet had no hair to cut.

In due course I was allowed to take her to Windham, her father bringing her in the morning and collecting her later in the day. I didn't worry – I would have done the same. Things would relax as she got older.

She was almost a year old before Connie finally saw her again, by which time her midnight hair and soft doe-like eyes were exactly like Connie's.

Christie was a determined little girl and walked early. When she fell, her mouth would set and her eyes narrow as she pushed herself from the ground, then she would not walk but run, I supposed to prove to everyone it had been a mistake. She would become either the bane of someone's life or their savior – possibly both.

But the most wonderful moment of all, came the moment Connie picked her up for the very first time and cuddled her. Christie pushed away from her, took a handful of Connie's hair and, looking her square in the eye said: "Mama?"

Connie naturally had hysterics and handed her to me. I also had tears coursing down my face. Christie wiped them gently away with her thumbs, then pulled her chubby little arm back as far as it would go and smacked me across the cheek. Since she rarely cried herself, she obviously thought everyone else should exercise a little self-control.

I never met a baby I liked until Matt and Christie. Gem, Addie, Edith, Robbie and Freddie were shadows in my mind – characters in a children's book read long ago. Deborah and Oliver? Well better not go into that. They had ceased to be my problem.

I never enquired into Connie's life with Oliver. I could gage what was going on by her pallor when I picked her up at the airport.

As I guessed she'd come to get away from it all, it would have served no purpose discussing her problems. Besides, she came against Oliver's wishes, so I could guess the atmosphere in their home every time she packed to leave.

She often talked about Matt though. He would cry when she left, afraid she'd never return as happened once before, when he was seven years old.

I think, in his early teens he'd have walked from California to Illinois to fetch her back. But she never would have left him again.

Even so, he knew nothing of Christie as he grew up, just as Christie knew nothing of her birth family.

One day, as we were standing at the window watching Julius carry his daughter away down the garden path, Connie turned to me and said:

"I hope Christie has an angel just like Trina – but not just yet!" she added, shocked by her own statement.

"I knew what you meant," I said. "No need to explain."

Julius had reached the end of the path and shifted Christie to his other arm as he struggled with the latch on the gate. She grasped him tightly round the neck, beamed at us over his shoulder and waved a hand sticky with chocolate.

"The day will come when she will choose to know you….and her father. I know it as I know the sun will rise in the morning. It will happen," I said.

"What was Trina's angel like?" she asked, still clearly absorbed in her original thought.

I put my head on one side and considered. It was an impossible question to answer, but for her I'd give it a shot.

"Weird," I said, "To look at he was absolutely un-angellike. Heavy set with blue eyes and an expression otherworldly in its sympathy – presumably because my baby was gone. No wings, not even a suggestion of wings. The thing which made him angel-like was that he was always wrapped in a softly radiating glow.

"He showed me my past: Charlie and Trina. Without words, he always assured me I would hold my little one again in my arms when he came to take me too. And I would know he was coming when I heard - quote – 'the music of the stars and saw his own child's first understanding'. I know - absolutely no idea either."

I'd slipped into a revery of my own. Describing him was difficult. His image was illusive, like a dream, his voice merely a whisper in my mind.

Somehow, this figment of my imagination had become the crossroads of all our lives.

Connie and I, Trina, Christie, Oliver, Deborah and all whose lives ours' touched would be swept forward by the unending love of this shadowy figure. I hoped I lived long enough to know him – long enough to see the stars, hear the music and recognize his own beloved child.

You can discover more about Grace Maxwell in:

'The Ultimate Link Trilogy'
by Lizzie Collins:

Book One:
Catch A Falling Star

Book Two:
The Twinkle in Pa's Eye

Book Three:
The Mountain Monk and Shadow Rider

All available for purchase from
Amazon
In paperback and Kindle formats

Printed in Great Britain
by Amazon